...ust.

...t was pure, passion-driven, desire-sparking lust. And this time, Lara wasn't in it for testing a little sample.

Her tongue slipped between his lips, swirling along his before backing out to dance over his mouth.

Letting her body run the show, she slid closer, her knees ...ngling down his thighs and her bare breasts pressed to ...is chest. Her mouth brushed his in a series of teasing ...isses. Each one grew wetter, hotter, more intense.

A response echoed in her body.

But she wanted more. More kisses, more heat.

Her fingers scraped across the velvet hardness of Castillo's shoulders, down the rock-hard curve of his ...iceps.

...sn't he a big one?

With a little growl of anticipation, Lara decided to ...o some exploring. She nibbled her way over that ...resistible dimple, dipping her tongue in before sliding ...isses along the hard plane of his jaw.

...h, he was tasty.

...ngling her body over the promising bulge beneath the ...lanket, Lara bit the chain around his neck, tugging the ...og tags aside with a jingle of metal.

...Now *this* was worth waking up for....

Dear Reader,

There is something so compelling about a military hero. A focus, an intensity that always draws me in. And, of course, military men tend to be in awesome shape. I've got to tell you, writing about guys with hard bodies is a lot of fun!

When Dominic Castillo first made his appearance in *A SEAL's Kiss*, I knew he needed a special story and a very strong heroine. One who could challenge his well-fed ego and keep him on his toes. Who better than the sister of his least-favorite person in the world? Lara is strong, confident and edgy, and she's more than ready to handle anything Dominic can offer up. Because this story is part of the Unrated! miniseries, it means a lot of what he offered up was pretty sexy!

I hope you enjoy reading *A SEAL's Fantasy*—and that you'll check out the earlier sexy SEALs: *A SEAL's Seduction*, *A SEAL's Surrender*, *A SEAL's Salvation* and *A SEAL's Kiss*. I'd love to hear what you think. Drop by my website at www.tawnyweber.com or find me on Facebook at www.facebook.com/tawnyweber.romanceauthor.

Hugs,

Tawny Weber

A SEAL's Fantasy

—

Tawny Weber

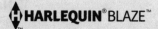

Recycling programs
for this product may
not exist in your area.

ISBN-13: 978-0-373-79815-5

A SEAL'S FANTASY

Copyright © 2014 by Tawny Weber

H HARLEQUIN®
www.Harlequin.com

Printed in U.S.A.

ABOUT THE AUTHOR

A *New York Times* bestselling author of over twenty-five hot books, Tawny Weber has been writing sassy, sexy romances since her first Harlequin Blaze book was published in 2007. A fan of Johnny Depp, cupcakes and color coordination, she spends a lot of her time shopping for cute shoes, scrapbooking and hanging out on Facebook.

Readers can check out Tawny's books at her website, www.tawnyweber.com, or join her Red Hot Readers Club for goodies like free reads, complete first chapter excerpts, recipes, insider story info and much more. Look for her on Facebook at www.facebook.com/tawnyweber.romanceauthor.

Books by Tawny Weber

HARLEQUIN BLAZE

COSMO RED-HOT READS FROM HARLEQUIN

To browse a current listing of all Tawny's titles, please visit www.Harlequin.com.

To the Sassy Sweethearts—the most amazing group of awesome ladies!

You all rock. Thank you for all the book love and fun.

1

THERE WAS NOTHING like a little bare skin to turn twenty adult men into drooling adolescents. Throw in a long, hard pole and a pair of glittery high heels, and they were a sad bunch of throbbing glands.

"Take it off, baby. Show us what you got."

As if she'd been waiting for those lovely and enticing instructions, the stripper offered a sharp smile and, quick as a whip, yanked her dress in half and threw it across the room.

Dominic Castillo listened to his brothers and cousins whoop and holler, half of them waving dollar bills as if they were winning lottery tickets and the stripper their prize. Once he'd have been right there with them, front and center. Not that he'd have to call out lame suggestions and wave money to get her attention. Nope, all Dominic needed was his charming smile to beat out all of his relatives for the sexy woman's attention.

But tonight his dollars were safe in his pocket and here he was, on the quiet side of the bar, sucking down a soda and wondering what the hell had happened to his life.

A year—damn, six months—ago everything had been golden. He'd been a kick-ass SEAL rocking his way up the ranks, carrying out death-defying missions and loving every second of it. Women flocked to him; he had a great family and a brotherhood of SEALs who had his back and kept life fun.

Hell, he used to wake up most mornings expecting to see a big ole *S* on his chest.

Used to.

Now?

He carefully shifted his head from one side to the other, glad his brain stayed put.

He'd gone on dozens of missions in his five years as a SEAL. His solid muscles and the scars were a tribute to his dedication to his career. He'd been hurt plenty of times. He'd dodged bullets, pulled shrapnel out of his boot and, on one memorable occasion, plummeted through the sky when the team's plane took on heavy fire.

Now he was sitting on his butt while his teammates carried out a mission he'd spent the past few months training for. All because of an equipment malfunction while he'd been fast-roping from a helicopter. When the cable snapped, he'd only dropped ten feet, but the impact had left him bruised, aching and sporting a severe concussion.

And feeling like a loser.

He blamed Banks. Lieutenant Phillip Banks, the biggest pain in the ass to ever earn the SEAL trident.

"I didn't think you were going to be able to make it until the wedding," Lucas said, watching the show with a bored look.

"Miss my little cousin's bachelor party? Bite your tongue." Dominic forced a smile for his big brother's sake. And, of course, to keep Lucas off his back. If his brother knew he'd been released from a doctor's supervision less than a dozen hours ago, he'd nag like crazy.

"You mean you didn't want to miss Lotta Oomph shaking her stuff," Lucas said, snickering.

"I've seen plenty of shaking in my time," Dominic replied dismissively, even while acknowledging that Lotta had an impressive shake. "Thirty states and eight countries, big brother. Can you top that?"

Lucas considered his beer bottle for a second, then tilted it and his head to one side. "Saw triplets pole dancing with their trained dogs in Reno once."

"Matching dogs?"

"Right down to their spots."

Dominic pursed his lips, imagining what that might have looked like, then gave his brother a nod.

"That's worth at least ten states, China and Mexico," he decided.

"I was in Mexico on a case two years ago. Gotta say, my job doesn't take me to many strip joints. Guess we know which one of us works harder."

As if, Dominic snickered.

Lucas ran Castillo Security. Providing private and corporate security for the past twenty years, Castillo was a family business, and it and their parents' ranch employed, well, the entire family. Four generations of Castillos lived in Seaside, the tiny town in Sonoma founded by Dominic's great-grandfather. From his grandfather Ramon to his little sister, Celia, they bred show horses, built security systems and provided bodyguards.

Except Dominic.

Dominic was a Navy SEAL.

The first, and so far the only, Castillo not pulling in an income from the family corporation. Which he'd worked damned hard for. When a guy grew up in a family as big as the Castillos', standing out wasn't easy. He'd never be as smart as Lucas or as sneaky as Marco. At six-four, he wasn't even as tall as Jose.

What he was was his own man.

The one everyone came to for help. Advice. Directions, even. He was hell on wheels when it came to directions. Handy, since he generally served as the point man and navigator for his SEAL team. Something he was proud of.

"Seriously," Lucas said, interrupting his mental back patting. "I thought Joe said you weren't gonna make it home for the party. What changed?"

Buying time, Dominic took a drink, the cola doing nothing to relax his aching muscles. A beer would go down sweet right now. A half dozen of them would go a long way to ease the pain racking his body. But the doctor had warned that severe concussions and alcohol were a bad mix for the next few days.

"The team is on a mission, I'm not. That means I could snag an extra week's leave and come home."

Lotta started her countdown, tossing her spangled bra into the rowdy crowd, then taking a few swings around her pole. Dominic made a show of watching, hoping Lucas would let the conversation die if he seemed fascinated by silicone so tight it didn't even sway as the stripper spun.

"Your team is on a mission and you're not?" Lucas asked, an intense frown creasing his brows. "What happened? Turning yellow?"

"I can still kick your ass." Dominic matched his brother's glower. Then he shrugged. "They didn't need me for this one. Plenty of them speak the language and I needed some downtime."

And a little distance.

There was no way in hell he could sit around the barracks, *resting,* while the team kicked mission ass.

The SEAL team was like a brotherhood. Every man

had the other's back. Every man knew he was a part of the team, each one vital to the success of their missions. They lived together, they trained together, they fought together.

Sometimes it was the best deal in the world. Sometimes it sucked.

Dominic had grown up with five siblings. He knew that life wasn't always smooth, that all relationships had plenty of ups and downs.

What he didn't know was how to deal with a guy who wasn't a part of the brotherhood. Who didn't fit, didn't even try to fit.

Especially when that guy was, thanks to his irritatingly stellar record, now the ranking officer on the team.

Who was so by-the-book uptight that he made Dominic sit out on a hot mission because the helicopter launched at 0700 and Dominic's medical profile said he was grounded until 0830. Hell, they wouldn't even have reached their destination by then. He could have gone if it wasn't for Banks's uptight ass.

Instead, the jerk had taken the team one man short and left Dominic feeling like a let down loser.

He freaking hated that guy.

"I'm thinking about transferring," he muttered.

His eyes wide enough to pop out of his head, Lucas dropped his chair flat, the front legs hitting the floor with a bang.

"Out of the SEALs?"

Dominic had taken a bullet, broken multiple bones and was currently sporting bruises down to the bone over three-quarters of his body, not to mention a concussion hangover and a weak ankle.

But none of them hurt like the idea of leaving the SEALs.

"Hell, no. Just, you know, transfer. Virginia, Hawaii.

SEALs are based other places besides Coronado. I might like to see a few, you know."

"Because thirty states and eight countries aren't enough?"

"I saw this act in Oahu once. Erotic fire dancer." Dominic blew out a breath, then fanned his hand in the air as if cooling off the memory. "Let me tell ya, a woman who dances naked with a flaming baton knows her way around big, hot sticks."

Lucas winced and shook his head.

"Sad, little brother. If that lame story is the best distraction you can offer up, you've obviously got something bugging you." He waited a beat, as if giving Dominic an opening to confess. But Dom did the advising—he didn't go looking for it. Finally, Lucas shrugged and lifted his beer again.

"You wanna talk, you know where I am," he offered.

Dominic nodded, even though they both knew he wouldn't take him up on it.

Not because he was such a snob that he couldn't reach out from time to time for a little guidance. But there was a reason he was the advice guy. In the family, on the team, with his friends. He knew stuff. Military stuff, girl stuff, sex stuff. Thanks to his nana, he even knew cooking stuff.

He stared at his drink, muscles aching and head throbbing.

It was a damned shame he didn't know what to do for his own stuff.

Two hours and three Motrin later he poured three cousins and one of his brothers into a limo. Patting the hood, he signaled the driver to hit the road.

Hands in the front pockets of his jeans, Dominic laughed as Marco popped his head out of the sunroof to serenade him with "Happy Birthday."

"It your birthday, big boy?"

He turned, grin in place, to watch the woman saunter over. Even fully clothed, Lotta still exuded sex the way some women wore perfume. Strong, heady and inviting.

"Nope. He's having a tequila-inspired calendar mix-up," Dominic told her.

"Too bad. I was gonna offer you a little birthday goodie," she said when she stopped in front of him. He wanted to tell her she'd be a lot prettier with about half as much makeup on, but didn't figure it was his advice she was interested in.

"I watched you while I danced."

Dominic looked down, noting that all it'd take was a cold breeze across her thin blouse to bring their bodies into contact.

Then he met her eyes, the hot interest and hard edge.

Message received.

"Isn't that a coincidence? I watched you, too," he said, giving her his most charming smile. He wasn't interested— yet another thing he figured he could blame Banks for— but he didn't believe in leaving women disappointed. He might not be going to give her a wild ride, but there was no reason not to make her feel good. In a fully clothed kind of way.

"Did you like what you saw?" she asked, her tone saying she had no doubts about that at all. She moved closer, so close that her ice-pick nipples stabbed his chest. Dominic had to wonder if she'd blasted those babies full of silicone, too.

"You do know your way around a pole."

"I do good work with long and hard."

"I don't doubt that."

Dominic looked her over again. He had a special appreciation for dancers. They were so damned good with their bodies.

Rethinking his body's aches and pains, he debated a little naked boogie with the stripper. He did a quick check to see if lust was stronger than bruises.

Nope. Not enough lust or too many bruises. Either way, he wasn't up for dancing.

Dammit.

"You interested in buying me a drink? I'll fill you in on some of my specialties."

The only reason the Castillo clan had vacated the club was because it'd been last call. Which meant the drinking destination Lotta had in mind was hers, his or of the rent-by-the-hour variety.

Dominic loved women. Strippers, dancers, teachers, nurses. He'd dated them all. His only requirement was that the woman take the relationship as light and easy as he did.

He'd heard plenty of times that his sex life was better than most guys' fantasies.

But if he had one particular weakness when it came to the fairer sex, it was for dancers. Ballet, jazz, exotic, tap. It didn't matter. There was something about a woman who knew how to make the most of rhythm that drove him wild.

But even if his body had screamed otherwise, he just wasn't in the mood.

"Sorry, sweetheart," he said sincerely. "I'm not drinking tonight. Doctor's orders."

She narrowed her eyes, clearly wondering if that was a euphemism. Then she gave a good-natured shrug.

"You ever get released from those orders, you come back. I'll do a dance just for you." She skimmed her fingers up his chest, giving him a smile that promised that it'd be a dance to remember. Then she tapped her palm against his cheek and turned to go.

Dominic leaned back on his heels, his own smile turning a little cocky. He didn't get guys who bitched that women were a pain in the ass. Himself, he'd never met a woman who wasn't a pleasure, in or out of bed. All it took was a little charm and a friendly smile.

He watched the stripper walked away, her hips swinging a hot rhythm beneath her short skirt. For one second he regretted saying no. Then, as he shifted his weight, his body sang out a protest.

A part of him, mostly the part cozied up behind his zipper, wanted to call her back. Not out of undeniable lust or anything crazy like that. More to prove he could still make her see stars and sing hallelujah, even if half of his body was bruised and the other half a step up from numb.

As far as Dominic's dick—and admittedly, his ego—were concerned, he was a man with many talents, all of which made women sigh with pleasure. He was better at sex when he was half-asleep, totally drunk and/or straight off a ten-day mission from hell than most guys managed to be even in their wildest dreams. He was damned good-looking—a blessing owed more to the fine Castillo genes than any effort on his part. He was a formidable SEAL, a savvy sailor and a weapon the U.S. Navy should be giving thanks for on a daily basis. Okay, weekly. He was wise—the team always looked to him for advice, hence his call sign, Auntie. He was smart and good with money.

All but the first were characteristics his own sainted mother recited to any single woman she found worthy. And all, including the former, were reasons Dominic saw as vital to his goal of staying single. When a man was as blessed as he was, it'd be cruel to limit his gifts to just one woman.

He watched Lotta slide into her Miata and frowned.

Maybe a good time was just what Auntie ordered. A hot ride would be a nice distraction.

It only took him a second to brush it aside.

Resigned, he watched her headlights fade into the dark night and sighed. It wasn't his bruises or irritation that made him a bad bet tonight, he realized. It was the same nagging feeling that'd been dogging him for the last couple of months.

Dissatisfaction.

What the hell was up with that?

Dominic was a man who made a point to be satisfied. In every way, every chance he got. Some might say he specialized in it.

So why the hell was he so damned bored?

Bored, discontent and frustrated.

All new emotions, and not one of them welcome.

Needing to move, wanting the rush of speed, Dominic straddled his Harley, tugged on his helmet and rode.

In the next three hours, he covered most of Sonoma. The wine country had a special beauty in the moonlight, but even that didn't help clear his mind. Finally, annoyed and still clueless over what he wanted to do, Dominic headed for the Castillo Ranch and home.

He cruised through the wide gate, its bronze *C* and *R* woven around the image of a horse, and throttled back. The sun was just making its appearance, casting a golden glow over the fields on either side, which meant the family was probably rising. Still, his nana slept late and her cottage was just around the bend.

The ranch housed thirty family members and a handful of hands and provided homes for a few, like Dominic, who needed their own place but didn't live there full-time. He came to a dirt road that cut through the emerald expanse of grass before curving behind a hill. His cabin was a few miles back. Remote, the way he liked it, and private. He spent most of his life sharing quarters. First with his brothers, now with his SEAL team. When he was home, he liked his space.

But he didn't take the turn. Instead, he barreled straight on down toward the main house. Ranch-style, it was big and sprawling, surrounded by gardens and manicured lawns. Lights glinted in the windows, especially, he noted, in the kitchen. Good. That meant Rosa was up, and likely making pancakes.

Dominic swept his motorcycle back behind the house to the wide driveway. Before he could cut the engine, his brother flew out the back door.

"Where the hell you been?" Lucas snapped, looking as if he was going to reach over and grab his younger brother right off the bike.

Just to be contrary, Dominic took his time slipping off his helmet and ran his hand over the stubble of his military haircut. He hooked the helmet over the handlebar, then swung his leg off the bike, shoved both hands into the front pockets of his jeans and rocked back on his heels.

"What's up?" he asked with a half grin. "I miss curfew?"

"Don't you answer your phone?"

"Not when I leave it on my dresser by mistake," Dominic said with a shrug. He didn't carry a cell phone on duty, and he spent most of his life on duty. So unlike his brother, he didn't hyperventilate without an electronic leash in his pocket.

"I've been trying to reach you for the last couple of hours."

"Here I am," Dominic pointed out. "You can reach me now."

"Before me, your buddy Brody was trying to reach you."

"Brody?" Brody couldn't have called. Petty Officer Brody Lane was on day two of a mission in Guatemala, taking down a drug lord who was pissing off the good ole U.S. of A. Lucas had met Brody a few times when he'd visited Dominic in Coronado or when Brody had tagged along on leave to the Castillo Ranch. "Dude, you want to play games, play them when I'm awake."

"No game. Your buddy called. He has a problem."

"What's going on? What's wrong?"

"Maybe if you carried your phone, you'd know."

"Cut the crap and tell me what's going on," Dominic snarled, worry tight in his gut. Brody wouldn't call unless the issue was major.

Chest to chest, the brothers glared at each other. Then, with a look that said he was doing his little brother a favor, Lucas stepped back.

"A mission went bad. Your friend didn't say that. He didn't offer any information except for you to call him as soon as you got back, no matter what time it was."

Crap. Hell, damn, crap.

Dominic paced, his boots kicking up dirt as he stomped from one end of the bike to the fence and back.

"How do you know he's on a mission?" he asked finally. "It could be anything. Hell, Brody might be calling for bachelor party advice, seeing as he's getting married next month."

Yeah, that was lame. Lucas didn't roll his eyes, but he looked as though the effort cost him. Instead, he gave a jerky one-shouldered shrug and glanced away for a second. Just one, but it was enough to make Dominic growl.

"Dammit. I told you to quit hacking military computers. That shit's top secret."

"I don't. I mean, not as a rule." Lucas grimaced. "Just, you know, once in a while, to keep in practice. Like maybe when I know you're doing something really dangerous. Just so I know to tell Ma to light an extra candle."

Holy crap. Dominic shoved both hands through his short hair, the thick stubble scraping his palms. For one second he envied his teammates who didn't have families. No nagging, no nosiness, no pain-in-the-butt interference.

"You get caught, you're going to prison," he finally said.

"I told you, I didn't hack anything top secret. Nothing military, even."

This time went unspoken.

"Then why are you claiming a mission went bad? Brody didn't tell you that."

"No, but he wouldn't call at three in the morning to get Lotta's number. I figured something was wrong, so I did some poking around." When Dominic just glared, Lucas shrugged again. "You said something earlier about plenty of people speaking the language. Since the only ones you speak are English and Spanish, I pulled info on a few hot spots in Guatemala that might require special-ized intervention."

Pride and irritation surged in equal measures. It was a good thing Lucas was as honest as the day was long.

"You are a pain in my ass," Dominic muttered. "That mission is top secret."

Top secret. And still underway. He clenched his teeth against the stirring of the hair on the back of his neck, warning serious shit was going down. Brody was sup-posed to be in Guatemala right now, blowing the hell out of a drug lord's compound, taking down his cartel and ending his reign of terror.

Not making phone calls in the middle of the night.

"When's he calling back?"

"He didn't say."

Of course he didn't.

"You okay?" Lucas stepped forward, looking concerned. He shot a glance at the big house, then back at Dominic. "Do you want me to do some more searching? See what happened?"

Lucas thought he could poke his digital fingers into a U.S. Navy SEAL operation. One that took place outside of the country, and was classified as a top-secret government mission. Dominic gave a halfhearted laugh, scrubbing his hands over his face. Likely big brother probably could. But that didn't mean he was going to.

"No. I'll wait."

"Want breakfast?" Lucas jerked his head toward the house.

Appetite gone, Dominic shook his head. He'd take the call in private.

"I'll check in later," he said, pulling his helmet back on. Even though he was on private property, if he didn't wear it, his mother would have a tizzy. He didn't bother with the straps, though. Just kicked his bike to life and roared off. Three minutes later, he shoved open his cabin door, threw his leather coat over the back of a chair and strode into his bedroom.

Yep. There was his cell phone. Right where he said it was. He snagged it off the dresser, checking even though he knew there would be no message, nor a return number. He debated for two seconds.

As far as the Navy was concerned, he might be on leave, but Dominic knew he was now on duty. Whatever was going down would take his skill, his talent and his absolute attention. He'd been up all night, barely slept the one before. It wasn't a part of his SEAL training that allowed him to sleep at will and awaken instantly, but his years in the Navy had honed that talent. He knew if the phone rang, he'd be immediately alert, even from the deepest sleep.

He didn't even glance at the neatly made bed as he headed for the kitchen.

He grabbed a box of cereal, a quart of milk and a huge bowl.

It might not be pancakes, but it beat the hell out of field rations.

He was on his second helping when his cell lit up.

It didn't finish the first ring before he had it to his ear. "Castillo."

"Trouble, Auntie," Petty Officer Brody Lane said in a low growl. His use of Dominic's call sign instead of his name made it clear this was military business. "You at home?"

"Yeah, took leave. No point sitting around like a pansy on light duty."

"You up to handling a problem?"

Shit.

"Name it."

"The Candy Man grabbed Sir."

Son of a bitch.

Lieutenant Phillip Banks. Call sign Sir.

Dominic's gut clenched, adrenaline rushing hard. His fist hit the wall before he even realized he'd lifted his hand. He didn't have to like the guy to be furious. Furious and, yeah, a little scared. Part of training for the mission had been studying detailed information about the Candy Man, as Pedro Alvarez Valdero had been tagged by the team. The man was a cold-blooded sociopath, his morals as low as his ambition was high. He specialized in drugs, torture and various forms of corruption.

If he'd grabbed Banks, that meant the mission had failed. The team wouldn't leave until they got the lieutenant back. And, of course, completed the mission.

"You want me to get him out?"

Brody's laugh was a soft gust.

"We got that covered. It ain't gonna be fast, though. While we deal, we need someone to defuse the repercussions."

Repercussions. Dominic stood at the window, glaring out at the soft morning sun as it bounced off the trees. The Candy Man was known for forcing cooperation by kidnapping and torturing his victims' family members.

"I thought Sir was repercussion-free," Dominic said quietly. Not that he was close to the guy, but he was sure someone had said the guy's parents had died, leaving him all alone with his uptight self.

"Tap *your* repercussions."

Castillo Security? If searching out Banks's family required those kind of resources, did Dominic really need to defuse the situation? Wouldn't the team have Banks out before it was an issue?

A heartbeat later, Dominic closed his eyes and bit back a groan.

Yeah. It was already an issue or Brody wouldn't have dropped the order.

"I'll take care of it."

"Top priority."

"Who do I report to?"

The silence was only broken by static.

Then the line went dead.

Dominic knew it wasn't a bad connection.

It was Brody's way of telling him they'd just crossed over into black-ops territory. This particular mission wasn't sanctioned, hadn't been green-lighted—or probably even heard of—by the powers that be.

If he got in trouble, he was on his own.

If he needed help, he'd have to find it himself.

And if he screwed up, he'd be tidily disciplined.

The military was funny that way.

Dominic dumped his bowl into the sink, only taking a second to rinse it. He knew Rosa would be by to clean before shutting the cabin up until his return, and dirty dishes pissed her off.

He grabbed his duffel, checked his wallet for cash and pulled his jacket back on. As he straddled the Harley, he punched a button on his phone.

"Lucas, I got a job for you."

GLEAMING JUST AS brightly as the glittering curtains and glistening stage, Lara Banks stood tall. Shoulders back, chest out and chin high. Sequins decorated the lush curves of her breasts and her shimmering skin reflected the multicolored lights.

Turquoise feathers floating around her thighs matched the ones on her headdress, a vivid contrast with the fuchsia lamé bikini bottoms and the gloves that stretched from her fingertips to the elbows she held bent at a forty-five-degree angle to hold up the feather fan at just the right angle to contrast with the rest of the girls in the line.

The music's tempo changed, and Lara swept the fan down to her knee. The vivid purple ostrich plumes tickled her bare flesh as she swished the fan high again and hitch kicked with the rest of the chorus line. She breathed through her nose, her cheeks stretched in a smile so wide her cheeks hurt. As hard as it was to dance in high platform heels, some nights her face ached more than her arches.

She could have taken a position farther back on the stage. She'd still have had to smile, but not as big. But stage left, smack-dab in front of the audience, meant she had to show not just her teeth, but a whole lot of enthusiasm. But the first position paid more, and the enthusiasm didn't have to be real.

Once she'd loved dancing. It'd been her life, her everything. She'd reveled in the training and embraced the discipline it took to make the body move in ways to which it wasn't naturally inclined. She'd donned her first tutu at three, tap shoes at eight and, dammit, a showgirl's headdress at twenty-two.

She'd given up her childhood for dance. Dating, the mall with girlfriends, even proms had all been happily sacrificed for dance. When push came to shove, she'd chosen dancing over her family. Not that they cared. It'd been eight years since she'd had contact with any of them, and she still wasn't sure if they'd noticed she was gone.

But life, being the big ole kick in the butt that it was, had made sure that all her passion, all her sacrifices hadn't mattered. A car accident four years ago had resulted in a bad break of her left femur and the end of her stint on Broadway. Fate and its wicked sense of humor had followed that up by sending her Mr. Perfect. And he'd been just that… perfectly charming, perfectly seductive, perfectly reasonable when he'd convinced her to drain her savings account and run away with him to his casino in Reno, where she'd choreograph his latest headlining show. Talk about a break.

It'd only taken her a week and all but her last hundred to realize he'd been full of shit. Well, that and walking into the room of the hotel he'd claimed to own and finding all of her stuff—and him—gone, and the bill waiting under the door. The only things he'd owned were a great ass, a charming smile and a BMW.

She'd learned her lesson.

Don't trust men. There was no such thing as a big break and when a pretty girl was broke, friendless and alone in Reno, almost every choice involved taking off her clothes.

She'd chosen to take hers off on stage wearing feathers and a ten-pound headdress, with twenty other women.

And since she was a showgirl who only danced the early shows and not a principal, she only had to strip down to the equivalent of a sequined bikini.

It wasn't Broadway.

But dance wasn't her passion anymore, so she figured that evened out.

As she strutted along the edge of the stage, her gaze skimmed the audience with disinterested eyes. She couldn't see past the front row, and most guys who ponied up the dough for up close and personal were card-carrying members of the pervert posse.

She found her mark, front stage left, shimmying in place while the principals gracefully mounted ribbon-covered swings, arching their topless bodies backward as the swings rose to sweep out over the crowd. Catcalls rang over the applause as the women shifted upward to dance on the slender bars of the swings.

One of the perverts jumped onto the stage and tried to grab a swing, coming away with just a handful of plastic flowers. The dancers didn't miss a step as a burly man dressed in black wove through their still-kicking legs to grab the guy and haul him off the stage.

Lara barely resisted rolling her eyes as the security man dragged the idiot away. Then a movement in the front row caught her eye.

Her gaze shifted to the left.

Oh, my. A little breathless, and not from the dance steps, her smile dimmed a little.

He was gorgeous.

Dark, intense and emitting such a gimme vibe that she was grateful that the sequins of her bra kept her nipples from showing.

He was big. Big enough to loom over the guys in the seats around him.

He was sexy. The kind of sexy that made her knees weak and her tummy shake. The kind of sexy that made her want to promise anything, just for one taste.

But she'd learned the hard way that every bite, nibble or lick cost a girl. And there was nothing she was willing to pay anymore. The good times just weren't that good.

Dance, she told herself.

Focus on the dance.

Next to her, Christi put in enough extra shimmy that the beaded fringe of her bra swung in circles. Lara was impressed. Used to working the late show, the statuesque blonde had a gift for swinging her pasties, but the costume top was a lot heavier than a tiny flap of fabric and a few dangling glitters.

Without thinking, Lara shifted her gaze to the sexy guy in the audience to see if he was impressed, too. But despite the blinding lights, she could tell his eyes were still locked on her. It was unnerving. Flattering. And one hell of a turn-on.

Let it go, she told herself. Thankfully, the music changed, and Lara led the chorus line in a swirling series of steps, upstage, then right, then back.

She'd seen plenty of gorgeous men in her time. Dancers didn't have to be pretty, but many of them were. Especially the guys. Of course, most of them were only interested in the other pretty guys, but that was beside the point. They were still plenty hot.

So hot wasn't worth wasting her thoughts on.

And sexy was pure trouble.

Now on the opposite side of the room, she felt safe looking at him again.

But oh, what a yummy mouthful of trouble he'd be.

It was probably the long, dry spell without sex that had her getting all wet and wild over a guy whose face she couldn't even see clearly. Maybe she should break open her piggy bank and hit the toy store. An adult toy might take the edge off.

And, more importantly, keep her from thinking about doing anything stupid.

She had plenty to think about already. She had goals, big goals. Goals she was this close to making a reality. And those goals required every single one of her thoughts.

So, sorry, gorgeous guy. None for you.

2

"LARA!"

Half the women in the dressing room were nude, another quarter stripped to the waist, but nobody batted an eyelash at the lumpy grease spot of a guy standing in the doorway.

"What?" she answered, tightening the belt of her robe. Some of the other dancers smirked at modesty, but she didn't care. For one, she figured her costume showed about as much of her body as she was willing to share with a bunch of people whose last names she didn't even know. And two, Rudy had a habit of following up his impromptu visits with irritating attention. A lot of the women were cool with that, since his attention usually came with better dance roles.

But not Lara.

"You busy tonight?" he asked, leaning one bony shoulder against the door frame and staring past her at one of the blonde principals who was cleaning the rouge off her nipples.

"Why?"

"Dana called in sick," Rudy muttered around a cheekful of tobacco. "You want her spot in the ten o'clock show?"

Lara grimaced. Her new textbooks had cost twice what she'd budgeted and rent was due in five days. The only way she was going to make it through this month was if she survived on ramen noodles and cold cereal for two weeks.

Of course, given the size of her costume, keeping the calorie count down wasn't a bad thing. But she had class tonight. It was her last semester, which brought her within kissing distance of her goal. And nothing, not even affording fresh vegetables, got in the way of her goals.

"Thanks, but I can't," she said with just a hint of regret.

She'd survived on less for longer.

And, hopefully, she wouldn't be worrying about barely making it paycheck to paycheck soon.

"Mistake," Rudy said, his gaze cutting to her.

"What're you doing in here?" Flo pushed past Rudy, cast a glance over the undressed state of her various dancers, then shoved the man out of the way. Once a dancer, now a stage mom, the statuesque redhead wore a beehive straight out of the fifties and blue eye shadow to match. "Get. I'll report you to Roberto, you sneak in here one more time."

"Didn't sneak. Came in to offer Lara a spot at ten. She refused. Stupid." He looked past Flo to give Lara a derisive look, then shook his head and walked out.

The door ricocheted as it slammed closed.

"He's right."

Lara glanced at the redhead, then shrugged. Apparently that wasn't a good enough answer, because the older woman stomped over, shooing dancers out of the room as she came. By the time she reached Lara's locker, half the room was empty and the rest were moving fast.

"I have plans," Lara said before Flo could poke at her.

"How long have you been here?" Flo asked, paying more attention to the costume she was inspecting for tears than to the woman she was bitching out.

"Two years."

"And you're not principal yet?" Flo adjusted the costume on its hanger, then pushed it aside to check the next one. "You're good. Better than most of the girls. You've got the moves, the talent. Your body is solid, sexy. Your looks stand out, even on stage."

As uncomfortable with the compliment as she was with realizing that the women left in the room were listening, Lara just shrugged and grabbed her street clothes out of her locker.

"So why aren't you headlining?"

"Maybe because I don't want to?" Lara said, tugging on her thong, then yanking up her jeans.

Christi gave Lara a sympathetic pat, then scurried around Flo and headed for the door.

Lara grimaced. She wasn't oblivious to the whispers that her answer caused. Nor was she blind to the expression of relief on more than one face. Dancers might put on the we're-all-friends facade, but it was as false as their stage lashes. And usually just as brittle. The chorus went out for drinks together; some even roomed with each other. But every single one of them knew that it was every woman for herself. If stepping over one to get up the ladder was what it took, then watch your scalp for stiletto gouges.

"That's the third time you've been offered extra. Rudy won't be giving you too many more shots."

Dammit.

Since Rudy wasn't likely to make another appearance so soon, Lara didn't hesitate to drop her robe. She pulled on her bra, the flowery lace stretching over her ample Ds as she slipped the satin straps up and snapped it closed. Unlike most of the women who were dressing, she didn't bother to check her half-dressed appearance in the mirror. She knew her boobs were full and high. At twenty-four, she had no worries about drooping. Her stomach was flat, and since she didn't have time to shower before class, it still shimmered with body glitter. Her long legs were poured into tight denim and as she pulled a light blue sweater over her head, the soft fabric draped and flowed to her hips.

"Roberto knows I need Mondays, Wednesdays and Fridays off after eight," she finally said. "I've got a commitment, and he's fine with it. Rudy's just playing a power game."

"Roberto might be the choreographer," Flo agreed, referring to the man in charge of the showgirls at the Silver Dust Casino, "but everyone knows that Rudy has plenty of power. Enough to trip you up if you aren't careful."

Balancing on one foot while she pulled on a knee-high stiletto boot, Lara sucked in a deep breath. She didn't need Flo's warning to know she was tiptoeing along the edge of blowing her job.

She'd run across plenty of Rudys in her days. She'd been dancing professionally since she was seventeen. Broadway in New York or casinos in Reno, it didn't matter. There were always power-hungry egomaniacs with hard-ons out to screw you over.

She knew it didn't matter if you were the best, if you were the brightest or if you had the most talent. She knew promises didn't mean a thing and that trusting anyone was an invitation to be screwed over backward.

This was the third casino she'd danced at since being dumped here in Reno three years ago. But dammit, it was going to be her last.

"I'll be fine," she said, zipping her other boot, then grabbing her purse and backpack out of the locker before slamming it shut.

She gave Flo a smile, rare for being real, and shrugged.

"I know what I'm doing, and I'll be fine," she repeated.

"I don't play by any guy's rules. Doesn't matter how much power he thinks he has. He can't mess with me."

Two minutes later, Lara had to sigh and wonder why life always sent her words back to bite her. Did she flip life the bird and tempt fate? No. Did she ignore hard-learned lessons and traipse down the same stupid path time and time again? No, no, a million times no.

But life clearly didn't trust her.

Lara walked down the long service hall toward the employee exit. The door was usually manned by a guard or two, big burly guys posted to keep the lowlifes away and make sure nobody played grab ass with the girls when they left.

Tonight the door had been left unguarded. And she was the only dancer leaving between shows.

Rudy might not be able to punish her officially for not taking his *generous* offer. But like petty men everywhere, he found a way to slap at her.

Message received.

And, she determined, her chin high, ignored.

She tugged her denim jacket on over the purse she'd draped from one shoulder to the opposite hip, automatically tucked her keys between her knuckles. She shoved the heavy door open.

She didn't make it three steps before catching the attention of the creep cadre, as she had disdainfully dubbed the men who littered the back alley of the casino. Dealers, dopers and desperate losers gathered in clumps. A dozen sets of eyes cut to her, then over her shoulder to the empty doorway. The nasty smiles made her stomach knot. But only because dealing with the creeps might make her late. At least, that's what she told herself. She wasn't a fan of lying, but sometimes a little fib kept a girl from turning tail and running.

For every step she made, the creeps slinked one closer. Her fingers tightened around her keys while she shifted her backpack off her shoulder so it dropped to the crook of her elbow, better for swinging.

"Yo."

Lara ignored the call just as she ignored the disgusting suggestions and lewd propositions. Her feet wanted to run, but she knew better. Jackals loved it when their prey showed fear.

"Lara Banks?"

She kept moving, her steps a little faster now. Twenty feet to the end of the alley and the road. Crowds, tourists, cops. She was almost there. Footsteps sounded like thunder as they came closer; the catcalls and rude comments were so loud now they echoed in her head.

Her breath hitching a little, she anchored her fist around the strap of her backpack and prepared to sprint to the end of the alley.

Before she made it three feet, a hand grabbed her shoulder.

Without thinking, Lara spun, swinging her pack with all her strength.

The only reaction the guy showed was a slight huff as it slammed into his belly.

She wouldn't get any help from the creep cadre. They were more likely to pull out their cameras and film the attack.

Fist high and ready to scrap her keys across his face, Lara froze.

It was him.

The guy from the front row.

Her stomach did a slow, twirling sort of dive, leaving fear behind and coiling into a deep, intense lust.

He was even more gorgeous up close.

And he was a creep who accosted women in an alley, she reminded herself.

Figured.

WELL, WELL. APPARENTLY little sister Lara had gotten all the looks in the Banks family, Dominic decided. And all the style. She had the same mahogany hair and green eyes as her brother, but the resemblance stopped there.

Her hair was short, a wicked angle that highlighted sharp cheekbones and exotically long-lidded eyes. And her mouth…oh, baby. Her lips were full and rosy, erotic enough to put a porn star to shame. Of course, that impression might be the result of watching her strutting her incredibly sexy body onstage for an hour.

He dropped his gaze to take in that body up close. It was definitely one worth getting personal with. She was tall, in her heels just a few inches shorter than he was, with most of her height in those long, sleek legs. The kind of legs made to wrap around a man and take him for a wild ride. Her jacket obscured but didn't hide the lush curves of her breasts. His fingers itched to move that denim aside and get a better look.

He resisted.

Not because she was glaring at him. Nor because of any stupid rules about her being off-limits because she was Banks's sister.

Nope.

He yanked his lust back, holding it in check.

She was his mission.

"Hi," he said, his smile pure charm. He didn't figure it'd take more than that. It rarely did. "You're Lara, right?"

"Excuse me," she said, moving her hand from side to side as if flicking him out of her path. "I'm in a hurry."

He'd been able to resist her looks, stunning though they were.

But that voice. Hello, darlin', that voice was pure sexual invitation. Low and husky, it was meant for dark rooms and silk sheets.

"You've got a second, though, right?"

She gave him a look, a combination of irritation and inquiry, as if she couldn't figure out why he wasn't listening.

He could have told her he was listening just fine. But her order and his wishes were in direct conflict, and Dominic made a habit out of getting his way. Especially when it came to beautiful women.

With that in mind, he amped up the charm a little and tilted his head.

"Look, I just want to talk to you."

"Right," Lara mocked with a roll of her eyes. "Talk. Sorry, big boy. I'm busy. Why don't you grab one of the girls on the corner? They're never too busy to chat."

He snorted. Damned if her smart-ass mouth wasn't just as sexy as her legs.

"We can keep it public. There's a diner across the street. We'll talk there."

"I'm not into talking, even in public," she said as she tried again to pull her arm from his grip. He didn't let go.

"Sweetheart, you just bared your all to a theater full of drooling guys. You obviously have no problem with public displays." A fact for which he was very grateful. He might not be planning to enjoy what she had to offer, but that didn't mean he wasn't going to appreciate its existence. Covered in shiny fabric or simple denim, the woman had a body of a goddess.

"My *all* was fully covered," she reminded him with frown.

"Not fully enough to diminish the fabulous view," he

corrected, his smile automatically shifting to flirtatious before he could stop it. Not that he'd have tried. After all, a goddess had to expect a little worship with a body like hers.

"I'm betting at some point, your mama probably taught you that look doesn't mean touch." She shot a pointed glance at his hand, still holding her arm. "You wouldn't want her disappointed, now would you?"

Dominic grinned. She was as clever as she was pretty.

Still, he didn't let go. Clever and pretty wouldn't keep her safe. He, on the other hand, would.

He just had to convince her of that.

After giving him an arch look, she tossed a glance over his shoulder. He knew there were a bunch of losers leaning against the back of the casino, all in various states of uselessness.

"Look, I've gotta go," she said, twisting the arm he held to the side so she could check her watch. "You have something to say, do it now. In thirty seconds I'll call the goons back. They might not be able to take you, but you'll have to let go of me to deal and then I'm gone."

"I need to talk to you about your brother," he said, trying not to sound amused. He knew from experience that women didn't like it when he wasn't intimidated by their threats.

Maybe she sensed that he was trying not to laugh, because she stiffened, her spine rigid and her chin lifting. She swallowed once, then glared and shook her head.

"Sorry, buddy. I don't have a brother."

"Phillip Banks. Lieutenant Phillip Banks. Navy SEAL."

She tilted her head, giving him a long look, then shrugged.

"Like I said, I don't have a brother."

Dominic rocked back on his heels.

It'd taken Lucas all of five minutes to pull Banks's family info. Parents deceased two years ago, sister estranged and living in Reno working as a showgirl. The house and ample family coffers willed to the eldest and only son, and all sitting in wait back in Maryland. From the info Lucas had pulled up, which had included Banks's sister's driver's license, home address and last known work address, the woman in front of him was none other.

"Look, sweetheart, I can't blame you for denying it. If I had Phillip Banks for a brother, I'd probably lie, too. But facts are facts, no matter how much we might not like them."

"I said I don't have a brother." With a stubborn look she tried to yank her arm away, then growled when his grip didn't budge.

"And I said you do. Why don't we go somewhere, get a cup of coffee and make a list of all the reasons Phillip Banks pisses us off?" Dominic saw the humor flash in her eyes for one second before her scowl buried it. He lowered his voice to a flirtatious whisper. "C'mon. I'll show you mine if you show me yours. It's a long one."

LARA HAD TO press her lips together to keep the grin at bay.

Long one, indeed.

No matter how long he thought his…*list* might be, she wasn't interested. Besides, when it came to reasons to be pissed, no matter how impressively big he thought his was—and she was pretty sure it was damned impressive—her list was *way* longer.

And any guy who could flirt with a woman while insulting her apparent relative definitely appealed to her. She had a thing for cocky guys.

But that thing tended to get her in trouble. So she'd learned the hard way that it was better—that she was better—if she straight up ignored it. Or, in unignorable cases such as the gorgeous guy standing in front of her, if she got the hell away as fast as possible.

With that in mind, she shifted her weight back on her heels, wrapped her fingers tighter around her backpack and prepared to swing again if he didn't let go.

Before she could, before she could even issue her warning, one of the creep cadre sauntered over.

"You okay?"

The temptation to say no, to ask for help, lasted about a second and a half. Lara flicked a glance at the gorgeous mountain of a guy holding her arm, then jerked her head at the four guys, indicating they should split. Even if they did manage to take him, the price they'd want for helping her was more than she was willing to shell out.

Nope, she'd take her chances with the gorgeous mountain.

She could handle him.

Forcing herself to ignore the mental images of the various parts of him she'd really like to handle, she cocked her head to one side, giving the hand on her arm a flick of her fingers.

"You've got an interesting pickup line, big guy. What do you call this? The Neanderthal approach? Grab a woman in an alley, grunt a few times about fake relatives and show off your studly moves for the local cockroaches?" She hoped her smile was snarky and not shaky, but her nerves were wound too tight to tell.

If she'd hoped to offend him into letting go, she straight up failed.

Instead, he shifted. His thigh grazed hers and while his fingers didn't actually move, she felt as if he'd just caressed her arm. His dark eyes turned molten, and his lips quirked into a sexy little smile. Heat swirled through Lara's system like a whirlwind, filling her body with longings and her mind with crazy thoughts.

"Tell you what, sweetheart. Why don't we get out of this alley and I'll work up a line you'll like much better." His words were silky smooth. So slick and easy that she doubted he'd ever had a single unsure moment in his life.

Now her nerves were racing for a whole different reason.

Eyes wide, Lara wet her lips.

His eyes dropped, amusement fading.

Lara's stomach clenched.

Not out of fear.

This was pure, liquid desire.

She'd rather be afraid.

But she also wanted out of the alley. She knew all eyes were still on them, that the creep cadre was only waiting for a chance to unleash their ugly.

"Why don't we go out front," she suggested after clearing her throat a couple of times. Out front were real people. Tourists and cops and traffic. She figured it'd take her three, maybe five minutes to ditch him there.

"Let's go," he agreed.

As if he knew she was going to bolt, he kept hold of her arm as they made their way to the end of the building. As soon as they rounded the corner, Lara relaxed. Like a lullaby, the sounds of traffic, people and music soothed. She glanced at the mountain out of the corner of her eye, then wished she hadn't.

He shouldn't look as intimidating out here.

But he was.

The dim alley lighting had hid his scariest feature.

Lara cringed, averting her eyes in hopes that the stained, dirty sidewalk would wipe the image away.

He had dimples.

Damn him.

Dimples on a guy—those were fatal.

"Coffee?" Dimpled and Gorgeous asked.

"What?" Lara looked up and almost sighed. She didn't have time for a guy like him.

It'd take hours, maybe days, even, to explore that body. Weeks just to get through her own fantasies about sex with a gorgeous, dimpled guy. God knew how long it'd take if he had fantasies of his own.

Nope. She glanced at her watch. She was already late.

She risked another look at him, noting the stubborn set of his chin and the determined light in those dark blue eyes. Blue, she thought as her nipples tightened. Blue eyes and dimples. The man was toxic.

Her mental debate took all of two seconds. She wasn't going to convince him to let her go and she couldn't match his strength. There was only one option left.

Seduce him stupid.

Depending on the street crowd and traffic to keep her from going overboard, Lara shifted. Just an inch to one side, but the move pushed her breast against his arm, her foot brushing his so their thighs touched.

She softened her stance, offering a soft smile, then gauged his reaction through her lashes.

His eyes flared hot, his gaze narrowing. He didn't take her silent offer, though. Since he clearly wasn't stupid, she figured he was either a gentleman—ha—or he was waiting to see how far she'd push it.

Far enough, she decided.

"Are you sure you don't want to meet somewhere more, um, private?" she murmured, wetting her lips and shifting so her hip bumped his at the same time. A zing of desire shot through her from hip to core—a hot, needy surprise. She let it show in her eyes, even more turned on at his instant reaction. His smile deepened and his body curved as if to welcome hers.

A guy who caught on that quick, reacted that well? What would he be like in bed? Could he read her needs as fast? Would he meet them? Lara loved the idea of fast, wild sex. So hot and intense that her brain couldn't have time to engage.

For a second, she forgot the reason behind her flirting. In that one moment, she was totally ready to blow off classes, quit her job, move across the country. All he'd have to do was get naked and worship her body.

"Why wait?" he asked, his voice seductively low.

Why, indeed.

Someone bumped Lara, shoving her backpack into her waist, the edges of the books jabbing her like a knife. She blinked, then frowned. Why? Because she had a life, dammit, and wasn't about to have it messed up because some guy was sexy enough to fog her brain.

Keeping that firmly in mind this time, she locked her eyes on his and leaned forward. He was so tall she had to shift onto her toes, touching the tips of her fingers to his chest for balance. And yes, because she really wanted to touch that chest. She had to work to not let herself be distracted by the hard muscles. Instead, she came within a hot breath of his lips, then gave him a sexy smile and a flutter of her lashes.

Someone jostled her again, and music pounded around them as the dancers from Circus Circus hit the sidewalk. Music and acrobatics followed as they gathered a crowd. Lara didn't have to check the time to know it was 8:05 and that she was late for class.

"We don't have to wait," she assured him, tapping her finger against that deliciously hard chest. It was all she could do not to follow it up with a pet of her palm. Since she figured good girls who resisted incredible temptations deserved a little something, she let herself lean forward that last inch and brush her lips over his.

Uh-oh.

He was so yummy.

Soft, warm lips that tasted so good.

His mouth shifted as if he were about to take control. Lara figured she wouldn't get a better shot.

Taking advantage of his distraction, she gave a swift tug and pulled her arm free. Whooping and hollering, the crowd of dancers reached them, providing Lara just enough cover to run. She sprinted into traffic, not looking over her shoulder until she hit the opposite side of the busy four-lane street.

Damn. He'd untangled himself from the feather boa and was already in the second lane. Biting her lip, Lara looked left, then right. Spotting a cab at the corner, she used her long legs to their best advantage. Ten seconds later, she threw herself in the backseat, panting to the driver to hurry.

Angling to her knees, Lara twisted to look out the rear window. The mountain was only two car lengths away.

"Hurry, hurry, hurry," she chanted.

The taxi driver must've looked in his mirror, because suddenly he laid on his horn, then, muttering, hit the gas, drove up on the sidewalk and around the lookie-loos still stopped at the light.

As the car squealed around the corner, Lara relaxed enough to wave, a little finger wiggle, at the mountain.

The guy wasn't even winded.

Nor, she noticed as she wrinkled her nose, did he look upset.

Instead, he only grinned and waved back.

"Lover's quarrel?" the driver asked.

"Something like that," Lara said, settling into the seat and giving him an address.

Nerves screaming with relief, she tried to shake off the adrenaline and settle her mind.

It wasn't fear that was dogging her, though.

She laid her head back on the cracked seat, closed her eyes and took stock of her body.

Nope.

That wasn't fear tightening her nipples or making her thighs tremble.

That was desire. Pure, lusty need.

Figured.

The first guy to turn her on in three years showed up now, when her entire focus was on—had to stay on—finishing her computer training and getting the plum internship the school offered. Which meant no distractions, no men, no sex. She'd made a vow—this time nothing was going to get in the way of her success.

It wasn't that vow that put him firmly off-limits, though.

Nope. Sadly, she'd ditch her vow in a heartbeat for a sexy guy. That's how she'd lost a plum role and effectively destroyed her career when she was dancing on Broadway. She'd called in sick one weekend to run off for a romantic trip. Snowy sleigh rides in the country, a quaint bed-and-breakfast with candlelight dinners and sex. Incredible, hot, wild sex. When she'd broken her leg, her boyfriend had left her in an E.R. two hundred miles from home and she'd been fired.

A year later, she'd given up a boring but lucrative teaching job at the dance institute to follow Mr. Perfect to Reno. A smart girl learned, after enough failures, to keep her vow and focus on the career.

Still, it wasn't the vow that had her sagging in relief over the near miss.

What put the sexy hunk with the gorgeous dimples off-limits was one simple fact: he knew her brother.

And anyone who knew any member of her family wasn't anyone she wanted to know. Even if he did have the good taste to admit that he'd deny a relationship with Phillip, too. That was guy talk, his way of trying to charm her.

"We're here."

Mulling and just a few breaths away from pouting, Lara grabbed her bag, glanced at the meter, then handed the driver the last of her cash and slid from the cab.

Phillip was a SEAL?

Lara blinked, trying to take that in. She'd known he was in the Navy. He'd been at Annapolis when she'd run away. No noncom status would suit a Banks, by God, nor would the heir apparent dare skip college. Two birds, one stone, that was Phillip.

A lot of people had been surprised that he'd joined the Navy. Phillip wasn't exactly the fighting type, the let's-serve-our-country type or the gung-ho-sailor type. But Lara had known better. Their grandfather, great-grandfather and a fistful more greats over the years had been naval officers for various countries, and he'd always been fascinated by the stories.

So the Navy didn't surprise her at all.

But the SEALs? That was a straight-up shock.

She tried to imagine her brother doing heroic deeds, part of an elite team in the special forces. But the picture just wouldn't jell in her mind.

Then she shook her head.

What did it matter? She hadn't seen her brother in eight years. And even then, they'd been strangers.

One thing she did know, though, was that then or now, Phillip wanted nothing to do with her. So whatever his buddy was up to, her brother hadn't instigated it.

The only thing worse than gorgeous, sexy guys wanting to lead her into temptation were gorgeous, sexy guys with their own secret agenda.

Lara settled into her classroom chair, ignoring the flirtatious wink from the guy at the station next to her and the glare from the woman on the other side. She smoothed a loving hand over the computer in front of her before sighing.

Nope.

She didn't need men, no matter how gorgeous.

3

THREE HOURS LATER, Lara stepped off the bus, shifting her bag into the crook of one arm while she dug out her keys. She didn't angle them like a weapon. Her neighborhood was run-down and on the cheap side, but it wasn't sleazy like the alley behind the casino.

It was the best she could afford. A far cry from what she'd grown up with, but a major step up from where she'd lived three years ago when she'd landed in Reno.

That didn't mean she was satisfied.

Soon she'd be making good money, she promised herself as she crossed the street. She might not be able to swing the snooty gated community of her childhood, but she'd own a home. Not here in Reno. She wanted a place in the country, where she could look for miles and not see another person.

Someday.

Someday soon.

Except that damned cab ride had cost her three days' meals.

She gritted her teeth. Leave it to Phillip to cost her more than she could afford.

She'd stopped blaming the sexy hunk about an hour after she'd escaped.

Sitting under the bright fluorescent lights of the classroom, she'd decided that tall, built and gorgeous was only the messenger. Between taking notes and coding HTML, she'd changed her mind about Phillip sending his friend. Maybe big brother had finally decided to clue her in about their parents' death. Not one to get his lily-white hands dirty, he'd probably asked his friend to pass on a message. Guys being guys, the dimpled hunk had probably agreed out of loyalty.

Phillip. Prince Perfect, as she'd called him growing up. She'd never have figured her uptight, upright brother to inspire that kind of devotion, but who knew. It'd been a lot of years since she'd seen him. Maybe he'd developed warmth, or oh, inspired miracle, even a little compassion in the last decade.

Or the gorgeous messenger was simply a card-carrying member of the penis brigade, loyal to any and all who sported the same equipment.

Men were funny that way.

Lara knew the only person worthy of her loyalty was herself. It hadn't taken long to figure that out—all she'd needed was for every single other person in her life to let her down before she'd clued in.

Climbing the steps to her building, she felt the weight of the day pressing on her shoulders. She'd danced the matinee and the early show, escaped a gorgeous mountain, then attended both class and lab.

She still had about twelve hours of homework before Monday night and eight shows to dance over the weekend. If she nailed this assignment, she'd have the top grade in the class. This cyberinspection program was the last of her course load and the school offered internships to the best graduating students with three top-flight security firms.

Six more weeks and she'd be working for one of those three. With a happy sigh, she rounded the hallway to her corridor. A year's internship while she still danced on the side and she'd be ready to go out on her own.

Lara Lee, Cyber Detective.

She grinned, then blinked. Frowning, she noted the hall lighting was out. Weird. The super was a lech, but he was a conscientious one.

No biggie. She was the second door, so seeing her keyhole wasn't a problem.

She'd just gotten her key in the lock when she felt him.

It wasn't his body heat that tipped her off.

Nope, it was the lust swirling through her system, making her knees weak and her nipples ache.

Taking a deep breath, this time she did shift her keys between her knuckles as she turned around.

"Do you always lurk in the shadows?" she asked.

"Hall light is out. Shadows are all you've got here."

"What do you want?"

"I already told you. I need to talk to you about your brother."

"And I already told you. I don't have a brother."

Not anymore.

"Lieutenant Phillip Banks. Of the Maryland Banks's. Parents were Randall and Ellen. Dad owned an investment firm and dabbled in politics. Ring any bells?" His words were easy, the look in his eyes as mellow as the half smile on his full lips. "Brother went to Annapolis right out of school. Top honors, joined the Navy as an ensign."

Her eyes narrowed, noting the slight change in his tone. His expression didn't change, but he didn't sound as though he admired those accomplishments too much.

"My last name is Lee." All her legal documents said so. It'd cost her a quarter of the small trust her grandmother had left her to make sure of it when she'd run away. Then, before she could stop herself, she asked, "Why are you running errands for this guy, anyway?"

His dark eyes flashed for a second before he gave a lazy shrug.

"Sweetheart, do I look like anyone's errand boy?" he asked, leaning his shoulder against the wall. He still blocked her exit. He was that big. But at least he wasn't looming anymore.

She couldn't resist.

She let her eyes wander down the long, gloriously hard length of his body. Broad shoulders and a drool-worthy chest tapered to flat abs, narrow hips and strong thighs. His boots were black, worn and very, very big.

She wet her lips and met his eyes again.

He didn't look mellow now.

He looked hot.

As if he'd like to strip her down and play show-and-tell.

Tempting, since she'd bet that'd be worth seeing.

"Sorry," she said truthfully. "I'm not the woman you're looking for."

DAMN.

Not for the first time in his life, or even the first time today, Dominic cursed Banks. The guy was a major pain in the ass. Even while captured by a psychopathic drug lord, he was still causing trouble.

Didn't it figure that long, lean and sexy was gonna be just as bad.

He wanted to grab her, haul her off to the nearest horizontal surface and show her exactly what he was looking for.

Which meant they'd both be naked, there'd be a bottle of warm body oil and a bowl of whipped cream nearby, and he'd be showing her with his mouth.

Insane.

He was on a mission. It might not be recognized by the brass, but it'd been handed down by his superior officer. So to Castillo, it was a duty.

She was his duty.

He'd never lusted after a mission before.

Not in the rock-hard-dick, blood-pounding-desire kind of way.

He didn't like it.

He wished he could say the same about the woman in front of him.

Her chestnut hair swept over strong cheekbones like a heavy curtain, ending at the sharp angle of her chin. She was tall, at least six foot in those heels, and all leg. All long, delicious leg encased in tight denim.

Tall meant he could gaze straight into her eyes. She'd looked like a sexy goddess on stage, her eyes heavily made up, false eyelashes glittering with rhinestones and her lips a candy-apple red.

But here, now, she looked even sexier.

He knew women. Oh, boy, did he know women.

So he knew that the only thing she had on her face might be a layer of moisturizer. No matter, she was great without it. Her skin glistened with just a hint of gold, her full lips were rosy and her huge green eyes were fringed with thick dark lashes.

"So if you're nobody's errand boy, what are you doing here, bugging me with some message I don't want to hear?" Those sloe eyes bland, she gave him a long look up, then down, as if she were assessing the goods. Since her expression didn't change, it was hard to tell if she liked the view or not.

Dominic didn't know why that fascinated him so much. It wasn't as if he expected to appeal to all women, but for the most part, they pretty much fell at his feet. Most offering any variety of promises—everything from sex to bearing his children to general worship. So this cloaked indifference was an interesting change.

Intriguing.

"I serve with Banks," he told her, figuring that said it all.

"Serve? Like, what? Drinks?" she asked, leaning against the wall and batting her eyelashes.

First an errand boy and now a waiter? She was either lousy at reading people, or she was hot on giving him a bad time.

His research said that their grandfather had been a Navy commander, that she'd grown up in Annapolis's backyard and that her brother had been well on his way to graduating the Naval Academy with honors when she'd run away. So he figured she was all about the bad time.

"Look…" She paused, arching one slender brow in question.

"Castillo," he filled in.

"Look, Castillo. I don't know what you want with this Banks guy, or what info you think you can get from me about him." As if sensing that he'd been about to interrupt, she held up her palm and shook her head. "Whatever it is, I'm not interested."

"I'm not here to get info, sweetheart. I'm here to protect you."

Damn. Dominic grimaced. What was with his mouth? He shouldn't have said that. He was just here to keep an eye out, not to scare the poor woman. Then he thought of the message he'd gotten while waiting outside her building.

Bad Ass says bad juju. Ugly on the move.

It didn't take much to decode that Brody was warning that things were going bad in Guatemala, they hadn't gotten Banks out and Valdero's men were likely to grab Banks's sister as leverage.

So maybe she should be a little scared. If that made her cautious, it was worth the info breach.

For one second, he thought he'd gotten through—her brow creased, her eyes clouded and her lips pursed.

Then she laughed in his face.

"Protect me? From what? Big burly guys accosting me in the dark hall of my apartment building? News flash, Castillo, you're the only trouble I've got in my life right now."

Her words were light, her tone amused. But Dominic knew how to read beneath the surface. He could tell that she'd had plenty of trouble before him and had probably handled it just fine.

Still, handling a drunk or a jerk of a boyfriend was aeons away from facing down drug-running goons who specialized in body decoration via knives and fishhooks.

Before he could tell her that in some form or another, he heard a noise in the hall.

Lightning fast, he grabbed her around the waist, lifting her off the floor. At her quick inhalation, he slipped his hand over her mouth to keep her quiet. He scanned the area. Four closed doors on the right, three on the left and a janitor's closet at the end. He strode toward it, the kicking, squirming bundle in his arms not slowing him down at all. He regularly carried a backpack that weighed al-

most as much as she did. Although, granted, it didn't try
to bite him.

He reached the closet, glad it was unlocked. Jimmy-
ing the lock would have required taking at least one hand
off the woman. Instead, he shoved her into the small,
cramped, dark space and pulled the door closed, but not
all the way. He peered through the crack, watching as two
thugs rounded the corner.

Damn, talk about timing. Not for the first time in his
life, Dominic gave thanks for whatever guardian angel
was watching out for him.

He glanced down at the thrashing handful of woman
trying to bite his fingers. Her breasts pressed tight against
his chest, a minor turn-on even through both of their jack-
ets. Damn, she was the perfect height. Pulled close to his
body, her face was level with his, so he had a good view
of the fury coating it. Her eyes spit fire and promised a
nasty enough retribution that he tightened his hold on the
wrists he'd snugged into the small of her back.

Power down, he warned his glands. Hot and horny
was fine in the proper place and time. A closet with gun-
toting goons outside looking for torture targets was neither.

As much to keep them safe as to get her out of temptation distance from his lips, Dominic leaned down to press
his mouth against her ear.

"I'll take my hand off your mouth if you promise to stay
quiet," he warned in a whisper. "Fair warning, you break
the promise and someone is gonna end up hurt bad. Before you decide, take a look through that crack and check
out your door."

Her glare didn't dim, but she did stop thrashing and
trying to bite him. Suspicion joining the fury in her eyes,
she stared for another second before shifting her gaze to

the crack of dim light floating between the wall and the edge of the door.

He felt it the moment she saw them. She sucked in a breath, whether to scream or cuss didn't matter. He pulled her back against his front, her ass snuggled up against his zipper and his cheek against hers. The move had a double payoff—she immediately stilled, and his dick was damned happy with the arrangement.

"Quiet," he whispered as she growled against his fingers when the goons finished busting the lock on her door with a swift boot to the hinge. It flew open with a crack. They didn't care about quiet. Guys like that were used to doing and taking as they saw fit.

One of the pair went inside while the other stood in the doorway, one hand inside his jacket. Since it was obvious he was gripping his weapon, Dominic figured Lara had clued in enough to the danger that he could slide his hand off her mouth. He didn't pull it away completely, though.

Just in case.

But she didn't scream. She didn't even cuss. She just gave a low hiss, sounding like an infuriated snake ready to strike.

"That'd be what I'm here to protect you from," he said, his voice so low it was as if he breathed the words.

Still cheek to cheek, she barely had to turn her head to look at him. Snapping with indignant fury, her eyes shifted from him to the door, as if asking what the hell he was going to do to protect her apartment.

"They're armed, I'm not," he whispered. "My job is to keep you out of their hands, not to take them down."

"Pretty sure if you do the latter, the former is moot," she whispered back.

"No engagement." Unless absolutely necessary. He'd

keep that to himself, since he was sure her idea of necessary and his weren't quite the same.

Slowly, he'd like to think reluctantly, she pulled away. His body instantly went cold and a little lonely without her.

Damn.

He gave in to the torment for a second, closing his eyes, leaning his forehead against the edge of the door and giving a deep sigh.

"We should call the police."

Her whisper pulled his attention back to the task at hand. He opened his eyes, peering through the crack at her apartment, with its door swinging drunkenly, only hinged on the bottom.

"Bet one of your neighbors already did," he said. "The goons know it—they'll be gone before the sirens get here."

"What…" Her words trailed off in a volley of cursing echoed out of her apartment. She puffed out a nervous breath, then finished, "Are they looking for?"

Before Dominic had to decide how he wanted to answer that, the men reappeared in her door. After a quick consultation, they headed out. Neither bothered to look around, clearly not giving a damn about caution.

Dominic, on the other hand, was careful to give them a solid sixty seconds to clear the hall before he eased the door open. Gesturing for Lara to wait, he paused only long enough to make sure she obeyed before leaving the closet. He didn't bother with stealth as he strode down the hall. Valdero's men weren't looking for him.

It only took a glance to be sure they were gone, but he still checked the stairs and landing, as well as the other hallways, always keeping the closet in sight.

A minute later, sure they'd left the building, he returned to Lara's apartment. What a mess. He shook his head before gesturing for her to join him.

Lara stopped in her doorway, shock chased off her face by fury. Neither disguised the grief, though.

Dominic grimaced. He knew he wasn't responsible. He hadn't brought the goons here. Still, he felt like shit over her expression.

"Sweetheart, you're safe. That's what counts here."

She wet her lips, looking around the destruction that'd once been her apartment. It didn't look as if she had a lot of possessions, which had probably accounted for the quickness of their search.

"What were they looking for?" she wondered aloud.

"You."

She bit her lip, eyeing a silk nightie in midnight-blue. He wondered how low on her hips that flimsy little thing fell and how much of her long, sexy legs it showed. He'd bet that was a beautiful sight. Shame it was currently shredded to pieces and anchored to her wall with what appeared to be one of her own steak knives. Her teeth snapped together with a loud click.

"Why?"

"To hurt your brother." He kicked aside what'd once been her telephone on his way to the window. Before he glanced out, he shot her a look over his shoulder. "Oh, wait, you don't have a brother."

She muttered something that sounded like *once a pain in the ass, always a pain in the ass*. But that was the only acknowledgment she gave his comment, instead crossing the room to check to see if the bathroom had been hit as hard.

He didn't need to hear her growl to know it had. This mess, it was a warning. Valdero's goons would be thorough.

"The cops are here," he said needlessly, since the thin windows didn't block out the sound of approaching sirens. "One of the goons is in the building across the street watching from the window."

"The police will protect me," she said, her fingers twining together before she shook them loose as if trying to toss off the nerves. "Won't they?"

Castillo turned, his careful gaze assessing as they swept the room. Then he looked at her and shrugged.

"Probably. But they don't know what they're up against, so whatever protection they offer might not be enough."

"You can tell them," she insisted.

"No can do, sweetheart. Missions are confidential. If my superiors want the cops filled in, they'll do it. But I've gotta warn you, they're out of the country for the next little while. A week, at least."

"But my apartment is trashed. They'll have to wonder why. They'll investigate."

He had to hand it to her—she didn't get hysterical or dramatic. Her tone was even, her expression calm. But he could still see the anger and just a hint of fear. Since she was a woman, his instincts said to soothe and protect. But training and experience told him that she'd be safer if that fear stayed front and center. So he went for honesty instead.

"Yep. Chances are the police will suggest you stay with a friend while they do." He eyed her living room, then tugged on his lower lip. "So, got any friends with disposable furniture?"

"You're exaggerating."

"Okay." Dominic knew perfectly well the best way to get a woman to do what he wanted was to agree with her. It didn't put them in a friendlier mood, per se. Mostly it tended to make them suspicious, and they ended up doing things his way out of sheer contrariness.

Was it any wonder he loved them?

"I'd guess you have about three minutes to decide," he told her, gauging the distance of the sirens and the traffic. "You wanna take your chances with the cops, deal with the results while they figure out what's going on, that's fine. You wanna come with me and be safe, grab your stuff. I'm outta here in two minutes."

Biting her lip, she glanced at the broken glass splintered across her floor, then at the window.

"Would you be taking me to a Navy base?" she asked, apparently forgetting she didn't know anything about what her nonexistent brother did for a living.

He could. No matter how many connections Valdero's drugs bought him, he couldn't finance his goons onto a secured base. But Castillo's role in this mission was still on the QT until the team notified him otherwise. Lane hadn't said what they wanted Castillo to do with her. Just that her capture would make their rescue of Banks much, much more difficult.

So...

"Nope. No base. Somewhere closer, safer," he replied. He glanced at his watch, and added, "You're down to a minute, fifty seconds."

He could all but hear her teeth grinding from across the room.

With a final glare, she snagged a duffel from the pile of her things next to the closet, then started grabbing clothes off the floor. The bag half-full, she hurried into the bathroom, where Dominic could hear her dumping toiletries in, too.

As soon as she came out, he grabbed her arm.

"Let's go."

"I've still got forty-five seconds and I'm not done packing," she said, yanking her arm free. She tossed the books she'd been carrying earlier into the bag, then ran into the kitchen. Dominic damn near dropped his chin when she pulled the oven door open and yanked out a covered casserole dish.

"Sweetheart, I'll feed you on the road. You don't gotta bring food."

She ripped the lid off, pulled out a slim laptop and a bright orange plastic box, adding them to her bag, then zipping it tight.

"I'm impressed. I didn't know you could bake yourself a computer," he mused, grabbing her arm tighter this time and pulling her toward the door.

"This isn't exactly a secure building," she said, tilting her head toward the shattered door as they passed it. She looked as if she was going to try to close it, then grimaced when she realized it was pointless. Castillo knew the cops would board it up, order the landlord to replace it. What was left of her stuff was safe enough.

"Stairs," he ordered.

As they clattered down the dimly lit stairwell, Castillo took stock.

He wasn't much on urban rescues. Most of his missions took place in the forest, the desert, the mountains. He was unarmed, had had time for only a minimal reconnaissance of Reno and had no backup.

They hit the alley at a run, but he held up a cautioning hand when they approached the street. Carefully, he peered around the corner of the building.

An ambulance was loading up a body bag.

He grimaced.

He'd wondered why the cops were taking so long to get to her apartment. Now he knew.

"What…" Her question faded into horror as she looked around his shoulder. Suddenly shaking, Lara sank into his side in horror. He could feel her breath shaking as she sucked in a harsh lungful.

"They did that?" she whispered.

Castillo's mental debate only lasted a second. Peace of mind wasn't going to keep her safe. The truth might, though.

"My guess is, yeah."

"We need to tell the police who they are, what they look like." She took a fortifying breath, then started to step around him. Castillo grabbed her back, his arm wrapped around her shoulders as he pulled her against his chest.

His eyes locked on hers, he slowly shook his head.

"Not a good idea. We can call in an anonymous tip later. After we've put some distance between us and them."

"But—"

"Sweetheart, you've got a hot body and a gorgeous face. Let's keep them safe, okay?"

The expression on her face was pure stubborn resistance. Then she looked over his shoulder. Her bottom lip drooped in a sexy pout that made Dominic hungry for a taste, then she wrinkled her nose.

"Fine. But I'm not happy about this."

"Take it up with your brother. 'Cause, let me tell ya, I'm not too happy myself."

Nope, not happy at all. The last thing Dominic had ever imagined was having the hots for the sister of a guy he couldn't stand. He knew all the rules between guys and girls, the varied nuances of dating a friend or coworker's sister. But seducing the sister of a guy he hated?

Dominic was clueless what the rules were there.

He looked down into Lara's big green eyes, then dropped his gaze to her full, seductive mouth.

Yeah. He was sure that whatever the rules were, he wasn't going to be able to resist breaking them.

4

Talk about a night going all to hell.

First she was hit on in an alley, then two creeps destroyed her apartment. And now, adding insult to injury, she was stuck in a fancy-ass hotel where the bellboys made more money in a week than she did all month.

Maybe, just maybe, she could deal with all of that. Maybe.

But doing all of that with a guy whose dimples made her wet and whose smile gave her insides shivers? That was a bad, bad thing.

Add the fact that his body was a work of fantasy. Big, hard, sculpted. She'd barely held back her moan of appreciation when he'd tossed off his jacket after they'd gotten to the room. Broad shoulders and biceps the size of bowling balls only made her wonder how big all his other, um, muscles might be. Big, she'd bet.

Lara folded herself into the plush easy chair, arms crossed over her chest as much in irritation as to cover her nipples, which were getting quite perky over wondering about Castillo's endowments. It was just as well that he was sitting behind a table. The only thing worse than her sudden obsession over his size would be getting caught checking. Once a guy knew you were thinking about his dick, he was all about whipping it out as if it was some kind of conversation piece.

Distraction, she told herself. Think of something else.

She winced when an image of her apartment filled her head. Nope, something else. Since she wasn't sure what she felt about that, it was better to ignore it for a while.

"If I'm the victim here, why am I the one imprisoned?" she asked with a wave of her hand to indicate the room. She didn't have to pretend to sound irritated. All she had to do was remember the state of her apartment, the state of her life and the fact that she wasn't currently putting in any time toward her twelve hours of homework.

"You've got a funny idea of what prison life is like," Castillo said with a laugh as he pushed back from the table. His plate sat empty, the steak and baked potato all but licked clean from it. He eyed her cold food with interest before arching a brow toward her. "Bet they eat their steak in prison."

"I don't see why we need to share a room," she said, ignoring his comment the same way he'd ignored her every time she'd complained about the room arrangements. Not that she could afford a room here, but that was beside the point.

"I can protect you a lot better when I can see you."

Okay, that was a good reason, she'd grant.

"They aren't going to find us here, though," she protested. Again. The man had a talent for ignoring her requests with so much charm, she'd look like a perfect bitch if she threw a fit.

She wasn't stupid enough to resent protection, even though she was pretty sure he was partially responsible for her even needing it. But there was nothing good that could come from her being locked in a room with this guy.

A room with a very big, very inviting bed. A guy this appealing was bad for her vow to stay focused on her goals.

This guy, in a hotel room? It was as if life was waving temptation in her face, challenging her to stay on track.

"I need privacy," she indicated. "I'm used to being alone. Having you here all the time is going to smother me."

"You look like you're breathing okay to me," he observed, giving her a long, intense once-over that made said breath lodge somewhere in her chest.

"How long?" she asked. Then, before he could dig in to her food, she got up, crossed the room and grabbed her plate. The look on his face was pure disappointment, like a little boy who'd just been told that Santa was fiction and Saturday had been canceled. Lara rolled her eyes, but unable to resist the cuteness, she slid the steak onto his plate.

"Thanks," he said with a grateful grin.

"I don't eat red meat."

He gave her a blank stare, then shook his head as if trying to shake off the incomprehensible words.

"No red meat? What's left?"

"Fruit, vegetables, white meat, fish, chocolate."

He shook his head again, then quickly stabbed his fork into the steak, sliding the plate close to him as if she might suddenly realize its appeal.

"How long?" she asked again. Not only because she had things to do, but because the longer she was with him, the harder it'd be on her willpower. It was like a dieter at Christmas. The first plate of cookies was resistible, but after a week, all of Santa's heads had been chewed off.

Nope, the less time they were together, the better.

For a second she considered suggesting the cops again. But she'd had enough experience with police to know that she was better off with a man who considered keeping her safe his mission.

"I have a life, you know. I can't live it in a hotel room with you."

Castillo flicked a quick glance up from the steak, his eyes holding hot promise before he dropped his gaze back to the plate.

Lara took a shaky breath, filling her mouth with a forkful of salad to keep herself from saying something else that might inspire that look again, just to see if it was as sexy as she thought.

"I figure we're here for a while. Can you handle that?" he asked, his look assessing now instead of horny.

"That depends on how many hours there are in a while." What was it with men and their stupid nonanswers? Her father had specialized in that. He'd play the conversation along for hours, days. Sometimes even weeks. Until he figured out exactly what her hoped for response was so he could be sure he went in the opposite direction.

"As soon as I get the green light from the team that everything is copacetic with that guy, Phillip, who you claim isn't your brother. Then we'll be clear."

"Copacetic?" Lara's lips twitched, so she shoveled in more salad to keep them busy. "I have to work, among other things. I can't wait for the return of the '70s."

"You're gonna have to call in sick for a few days," he said, eyeing the baked potato still on her plate.

Lara cut off a chunk, scooped it through the sour cream, then popped it into her mouth with a defiant smile, even as she shook her head.

"I don't call in sick. In the first place, I'm not sick, so that'd be lying. In the second place, I can't afford to miss work. You wanna play bodyguard, you can do it while I'm on stage."

"You can miss a few days."

Said like a typical man. Her eyes flicked to his leather jacket while her mind flashed to the wad of cash he'd shelled out for this room.

"You grew up with money, didn't you?" she said.

"I make my own way. Besides, if research is right, you grew up with a hell of a lot more than I did."

Touché. Lara grimaced.

"Let's put it this way—every paycheck is vital at this juncture of my life. Besides, if I don't show up, I'll lose my spot in the chorus line."

"Can't be helped. You're vulnerable there and I'm not letting some goon with a knife fetish stare at you in all your seminaked glory. He sees all that gorgeous flesh and he might not be able to control himself."

"I'm pretty sure I've had worse staring at all my naked flesh before," she said, slanting him an ironic look to remind him that he'd been staring himself that very afternoon.

Castillo's smile was as unapologetic as his shrug.

"Think of it this way, the nights are getting cooler and by staying here safe with me, you'll be able to keep all your clothes on. I'm good for you, see? Keeping you from maybe catching a cold."

"Oh, no, you don't," Lara snapped, pushing away from the table as the frayed edges of her temper shattered. "Look, buddy, I've been on my own for many years now. Maybe I've made a few mistakes here and there—here being a major one, by the way. But for the most part I've done a damned good job of taking care of myself. I don't need some macho man with a bodyguard complex telling me what I need."

Did he look abashed? Did he apologize?

Hell, no.

Castillo just pulled an intrigued face, his fingers tapping a mellow rhythm against his empty plate as he leaned back in his chair and gave her a long, contemplative look.

"It's for your own good," he finally said, his avuncular smile echoing the arrogance of his tone.

Lara could have sworn she felt her head explode. She slammed her plate on the small table hard enough that the bud vase shook and the rose dropped a petal. She gouged her fists into her hips and leaned forward so her face was inches from his.

"And you know what's good for me? Because, why? Is it that big bad man thing? Like li'l ole me, poor penisless thing that I am, doesn't have a clue?"

Breathing in with a hiss, she stepped back and waited for his apology.

The son of a bitch nodded.

Lara's fists clenched. Then she noticed the amusement on his face making his dimple wink.

Hell. She winced. He'd been winding her up. And she'd walked right into it. She should know better. The few times in her life that Phillip had pretended to be her brother instead of the reigning prince of the house, he'd done the same thing. She'd hated it then, too.

Since dumping his school medals in the flower garden then turning on the sprinklers the way she had with her brother wasn't an option, Lara decided on a more grown-up form of revenge.

She'd spent enough of her life on stage, using her body to make a point. So all it took was a shift of her hips, a tilt of her chin and twisting just a little to thrust her breasts out. Her bottom lip pouted and she let her gaze turn slumberous.

The message was sex.

Castillo's eyes narrowed, interest flaring hot and intense

in the blue depths. His smile sharpened, more seductive than amused now. He still leaned back in the chair, but his body tensed, as if he were about to leap up and grab her.

Good.

Lara shifted, leaning her hip against the table and casually running her finger over her bottom lip before giving a deep sigh. His eyes didn't drop so much as meander their way down from her face to her throat to her breasts. His gaze was electric, so arousing she felt as if he'd brushed his fingers over her nipples, bringing them to attention.

"You know, it'd be a terrible shame to underestimate me," she told him, keeping her voice low and just-out-of-bed husky.

"Believe me, I don't underestimate a single thing."

"Hmm, maybe not." She moved forward, sliding around the table so her butt was against the edge and her front within touching distance of his.

Before she could decide if she was going to plop herself down in his lap or grab his shirtfront and pull him to his feet, Castillo rose.

The man towered over her. For a woman who stood five-ten barefoot, that was a rare thing. Between his height and his bulk, he made her feel positively petite. Fragile and ladylike, even.

Liking it, Lara tilted her head in challenge. She hadn't formed much of a plan when she'd made her first move. Just to make him uncomfortable.

Now all she wanted was to see how he tasted, how he felt. To find out what he could make her feel.

"You might want to factor this into your estimating," she told him before sliding her hands up his chest and linking them behind his neck.

Her eyes locked on his dark gaze, Lara stood on tiptoe to brush her lips over his.

Oh. He tasted so good. Sweet and sexy at the same time. His mouth was soft, his bottom lip tempting her. Unable— unwilling—to resist, she gave it a quick nip before sooth- ing it with her tongue.

It was like lighting a stick of dynamite.

One second he was calm, almost mellow.

The next he exploded.

Castillo's hands wrapped around her waist, pulling her tight against his body. Oh, man, what a body he had— hard, big and enticing. Lara had to force herself not to rub against him like a cat in heat.

She wasn't sure how long she'd be able to hold out, though.

He took over the kiss, his tongue thrusting between her lips, fast and furious. Hot and wild.

Lara's chest grew tight because she was breathing so hard. Her thighs trembled, damp need pooling between her legs, her core aching for his touch.

Danger, her mind screamed. It took it a few rounds, though, before the warning penetrated the passion fog- ging her brain.

Screw danger. Her lips moved under Castillo's; her tongue tangled with his in a wild dance. Her fingers roamed up and down the hard plane of his glorious chest. The soft fabric of his shirt skimmed her knuckles, mak- ing her impatient to get it off him.

He was so yummy. It was like licking a chocolate foun- tain, sucking on a salted caramel, all with the promise of orgasmic delights yet to come and all of them calorie-free, pleasure-inducingly incredible.

Impatient, need scrambling through her as wet heat coiled low and tight between her thighs, she flicked a but- ton open to get his shirt out of her way.

She'd only unbuttoned two more when his fingers closed

over hers. Castillo's mouth was still hot, his tongue still dancing with hers. But he changed the pace. Now it was soothing. Her heart rate slowed from frantic need to mellow desire. She'd never ridden passion like a roller coaster before, but this man made her want to ride again and again.

So achingly slow, he pulled his mouth from hers. His lips brushed softly over hers once or twice before he lifted his head.

Lara's breath shuddered, her insides actually shaking with need. Her lashes fluttered a couple of times before she forced them up so she could look at him.

His eyes were hot, his dimples so sexy she couldn't resist sliding her thumb over one.

"Believe me, I'm not holding your not having a penis against you," he promised in a husky tone. His breath warmed her face, his body hot against hers. Her shaky insides turned molten, desire washing over her in huge, crashing waves.

Then, shocking the hell out of her, he set Lara aside. Actually lifted her by the elbows and moved her a half foot away from him. She was tempted to reach out and grab him, just to prove that she could. Then she remembered that she was trying to make a point.

She just wished she could remember what it was. She sucked in a deep, cleansing breath, hoping the air would reignite her brain.

"But as good as that was, I'm here to keep you safe," he said, the warmth leaving his tone as if he'd just flipped a switch.

Sexy guy to military mannequin, she realized, trying not to grind her teeth in frustration. Then she remembered the point of that kiss. To punish him for laughing at her.

Ah, life and its little jokes at her expense.

Lara pushed her hand through her hair, wondering when she'd learn.

Instead of punishing him, she'd made a fool of herself. Now she looked like a sex groupie, his for the plucking. Worse, Lara was pretty sure if he wanted to pluck her, she'd dive right in, desperate to feel more of the magic he'd been wielding over her body.

"Right. Safe," she said, not sure if she was more irritated at his macho act or sexually frustrated. It didn't matter. Both sucked. "And if I don't want your protection?"

Castillo's face was blank for a second, looking like a soldier or sailor or whatever he called himself. Then, in the blink of an eye, his expression shifted. Calming charm. She figured it was just as effective a weapon as whatever guns he played with. As long as his opponent was female.

He slid into the chair opposite her, oddly graceful for a guy as huge as he was.

Don't think about size, she warned herself. She was glad he was sitting, though, and almost patted the table in appreciation for it blocking her view of his lap.

"Look, I'm not trying to mess up your life. This really is for your own good. There are guys out there who will hurt you in a major way. I have orders to prevent that. So why don't you settle in, call it a holiday and enjoy yourself?" Castillo flashed those dimples, his tone so reasonable that Lara almost nodded before the words hit her brain.

Seriously? She was an assignment to him, and that was it? How ego smashing was that? Here she was, her panties wet and her lips still tingling from his kiss. She was sneaking peaks at his package and weaving lusty fantasies about the various ways she'd like to use his body as a sex toy. And he saw her as an *obligation.*

Not sure if she wanted to throw a tantrum or strip naked and show him what he was missing, Lara threw herself into the chair instead. She bit her lip, then figuring she'd rather he not know how crazy horny he'd gotten her before easily stepping back, Lara made a show of eating her cold potato.

She debated her options. Staying here in a hotel room with the guy was the suckiest one. But what were her choices?

He said she was in danger but he hadn't said why. Because, what? Her brother was a jerk?

Every minute that ticked by eked away a little more of the horror that'd been her apartment experience. Sure, some creeps had trashed the place. And yeah, someone had been hauled out. But that didn't mean the creeps had actually hurt someone. There were old people in the building. But Castillo had rushed her out so fast, spouting his conspiracy theory so convincingly, that she hadn't verified a damned thing.

She made a show of eating, sneaking peeks at the man across from her every few seconds. If he was peeking at her, he had a lot of skill at hiding it. Instead, all of his attention was on his phone, reading whatever the hell was on there. Maybe more instructions on how to mess with her life.

Not gonna happen, Lara decided. She set the fork down, determined to take off at the first opportunity. Those goons might be something of a threat. But she figured Castillo was a bigger one. The goons might try to hurt her. But the gorgeous guy with dimples across from her? A guy with a mouth and hands like his could devastate her without any effort at all.

DOMINIC SCROLLED THROUGH his messages, putting all his focus on ignoring the woman sitting across from him.

He'd never blown a mission. And as much as he appreciated women in all their various forms of entertainment, he'd never let one interfere while he was on duty.

Hell, he couldn't remember ever even thinking about one while he was in uniform. Maybe that was the problem—he was in civilian clothes and not officially on duty. Sure, his dog tags were hanging from his neck, but clearly they weren't enough. Pursing his lips, he tapped a few keys on his phone, looking for a surplus store nearby. A camo tee, a cap, maybe they'd help.

Better yet, he could get a tent and wrap the sexy brunette in it. Maybe she'd be less tempting buried in yards of fabric.

Mocking that thought, his brain immediately went to a vision of Lara on stage, dancing in feathers and a few scraps of fabric. Long silky legs, her flat abs glittering and her lips glistening wet.

Those lips that tasted like sugar, addicting and delicious.

That body, a perfect fit against his with all her exquisite curves and tempting angles.

His body hardened, dick pressed painfully against his zipper. Hell, he'd barely kissed her. His hands hadn't left her waist. But he was reacting as if she'd gone down on him while she was wearing thigh-high stiletto boots and glossy red lipstick.

Nope. He figured he could wrap her in a submarine and she'd still be pure temptation.

"Yo, soldier boy. I said this isn't going to work for me," Lara said.

Her irritated tone made Dominic want to grin, but he manfully held back.

"Sailor, actually."

"What?"

"Navy. Sailor," he pointed out, waiting for her to get

it. He took her eye roll as understanding, then continued. "What d'ya need? I'll take care of it for you."

It was the least he could do, considering the varied sexual fantasies he was having about her.

"Privacy, for one."

"You want the bedroom, I'll hang here in the sitting area." Wishing he'd popped for a bigger suite. One that had a bedroom door with a big lock.

"Why don't you hang out in the hallway? Isn't that what bodyguards do? Stand with their back to the door and glower at passersby?"

Dominic ruefully shook his head. Damned if he didn't like her. Liking was okay, he decided. It was the lusting part that was off-limits.

"The bedroom is all yours," he said again. Then, figuring he'd better make it clear to both of them since it was almost midnight, he went to the closet, grabbed the spare pillow and blanket and tossed them on the couch.

"You're too tall to sleep comfortably on that," she pointed out. He noted that she didn't offer up the bed. Just as well, since he didn't know how strong his resistance would be if she did.

"No worries," he said with a shrug. "It pulls out into a bed."

"Those are always miserably uncomfortable," she said with a smile that said she didn't care if he slept on a bed of nails. He didn't bother telling her that a lumpy pullout, or a bed of nails, would be less uncomfortable than sleeping less than thirty feet from her.

He remembered that tiny scrap of silk knifed to her wall, then slanted a glance at her duffel. He hoped like hell she didn't have more of those little babies with her. Just imagining her in one was going to cost him hours of sleep.

"I need internet," she said, grabbing her duffel and heading for the bedroom. "I'm charging it to the room."

"No email," he warned automatically.

"I can conceal my location if I need to." She shot him a look over her shoulder.

Sure she could.

"No email," Dominic said again. He tossed the blanket and pillow on the couch, figuring it wasn't worth pulling out. He wasn't sleeping anyway. Not while on duty. He figured someone on the team would check in within the next six hours. If he didn't hear in twelve, he and his assignment would be heading to San Diego. He'd find out more on base than he could here in Reno.

"You might want to call your boss, tell them you're outta commission for the next few days," he said. Since she'd already shared her opinion of missing work, he held up one hand to halt a repeat. "Just the weekend. Your brother will cover any wages you lose. Deal?"

Green eyes narrowed in consideration, Lara pursed her lips in a way that made him want to groan, then nodded her head.

"Missing a weekend will damage my position. I want time and a half."

"Fine by me." And please, let him be there when she told Banks. Grinning, Dominic handed her his cell phone. "Make the call from this. It's secure, won't show on their caller ID."

"You watch too many spy movies." Still, she took the phone. After giving it a quick inspection, she made the call.

From Dominic's position as an interested listener, the call didn't go well. Lara's expression never changed, her tone didn't alter. But her body tensed. Shoulders shifted as though she was shaking something off. Her fingers flexed, then stilled and she gave the smallest sigh, which did amazing things for her shirt. Her breasts shifted, the fabric at her waist lifting to show a hint of skin. He'd already seen her in little more than a bikini and feathers, so that sneak peek of her flat belly shouldn't be a turn-on.

Officially or not, he was on duty. So he was going to pretend that he wasn't affected. He just had to send the *at ease* memo south to his dick.

It wasn't listening, but thankfully she ended the call and looked at him before it could get any ideas. Well, any *more* ideas.

"Trouble?"

She pulled a face, then tossed him the cell phone.

"Nothing to worry about. Rudy's having a fit, but I talked to Flo and she'll handle things."

"And Rudy is?"

Lara shrugged. "Let's just say Rudy isn't a fan."

"Want me to rough him up?" Dominic asked, the same offer he'd put out to his sisters and female cousins numerous times. None of them had ever taken him up on it, but it always made them feel better.

Lara didn't look as if it worked for her. Instead of looking comforted, she seemed skeptical.

"Do you think you could?"

Oh, ye of little faith.

"Pretty sure I can handle him, no matter how big he is," Dominic assured her. He mentally flipped through the list of enemies he'd taken out, such as the huge Turk with an M1 Garand he'd disabled with just his feet. So unless her coworker was sporting a Gatling gun, Dominic was good to go.

He managed to keep that to himself, though.

Barely.

"Rudy?" She shrugged, her eyes shifting down his body, then back up with an assessing arch of her brow. "He's about five-seven, weighing in at a lumpy one-sixty and tends to tilt forward, since twenty of those pounds are hanging over his belt."

There was a ringing in his ears. The sound of his jaw hitting the floor, maybe?

Was she serious?

He searched her face for signs that she was joking, but there weren't any. For the first time, he saw the resemblance to Banks. Not in looks, though.

Nope. It was the tiny ball of irritated fury she lit in his gut.

"You do realize I'm a Navy SEAL, right? A highly trained, special forces military machine."

"So you keep saying."

"You want proof?" He had his hand halfway to his collar to pull out his dog tags before he stopped himself. What was it about this family that made him feel as though he had to prove himself?

Stupid.

Dominic tried to shake off the irritation—something he wasn't used to feeling with women. He needed space. The hotel room only supplied about thirty possible feet of distance, but he'd take it.

"It's late. Get some sleep," he ordered. So he could get some peace of mind.

5

MORNING? ALREADY?

Mornings sucked.

Lara squinted, not willing to actually commit to opening her eyes yet. Not until she knew how early it was and if it was even necessary to wake yet.

Dim lights made waking debatable. But her body insisted that she really should get up. But that didn't mean waking, in Lara's opinion.

Skilled at functioning in a near-sleep state, she shoved the blankets off and swung out of bed. Her brow furrowed when her toes hit a warm, toasty floor, but she didn't question it. Hey, maybe someone had found a way to heat the worn linoleum in her bedroom.

It wasn't until she hit a wall with her forehead that she remembered that she wasn't home.

Hotel.

Castillo.

Hot, sexy bodyguard.

Damn.

She adjusted course, using her hands this time to prevent any more walls.

No lights. Lights were a part of morning.

And mornings sucked.

In the bathroom, Lara slid back into her half-asleep fog.

Then she realized she didn't even have a toothbrush.

Growling, she felt around the counter until she found a tube of complimentary toothpaste. Tossing the cap on the counter, she squeezed out a stream onto her finger and made do.

Still with her eyes closed.

Rinse, spit, a quick wash of her hands and she was ready to go back to bed.

Her eyes slitted open just enough to see the hazy shadow of her toes, she felt her way to the door and stumbled out. Was the bed to the left or right?

Left.

Maybe?

She stumbled along, humming her usual start-of-the-day mantra.

Mornings sucked.

Mornings sucked.

Mornings suc—

Her toes slammed into something. Hard.

She choked on a garbled scream as she flew toward the floor.

Oh, hell. She squeezed her eyes tight. She knew from experience that watching didn't make the impact hurt any less.

Two hands banded her waist, fingers digging into her flesh, holding her aloft.

Lara's eyes flew open.

"What the…"

Oh.

Castillo.

On the floor.

Her hands crawled across his bare shoulders.

Castillo, on the floor *naked*.

Oh, my.

Her blurry gaze locked on her hand, the contrast of her pale fingers against the golden silk of his skin.

Yummy skin.

Yummy, soft skin that looked as if it'd taste really good.

Really, really good.

Lara swallowed, wondering where all her spit had gone.

She didn't even have enough to wet her lips.

Which meant she wouldn't have any for tasting.

Dammit.

Her knees hit the floor, one on each side of blanket-covered hips. His hips.

If she thought she could make her eyes focus, she'd have peered between their bodies to see if he was naked all the way down. No worries. She'd rather find out by feel, anyway.

"Hi." His voice husky, Castillo's fingers tightened on her waist.

"Huh?" she mumbled.

"You were right. I didn't fit on the couch."

"Eh?"

She knew he was talking, but her brain just wasn't engaging. It wasn't sleep that was shutting her down this time, though.

Nope.

Lust.

It was pure passion-driven, desire-sparking lust.

Yum.

Did he taste as good as he looked?

She bent her head to his mouth, running her tongue along the seam.

Mmm, he tasted mighty good.

Good enough to make her hungry for more.

"Hey." He hadn't sounded surprised when she dove onto his body, but he did now.

"Hey back," she murmured, wriggling a little to get more comfortable.

Then, before he could follow that *hey* up with anything annoying, she bent again for another taste.

This time she wasn't in it for a testing little sample.

Her tongue slipped between his lips, swirling along his before dancing back out to dance over his mouth.

His fingers tightened on her waist. His body tensed beneath her fingers. But he didn't respond.

Oh, a challenge.

Letting her body run the show, she slid closer, her knees angling down his thighs and her breasts pressed to his chest. Her mouth brushed his in a series of teasing kisses. Each one grew wetter, hotter, more intense.

A response echoed in her body.

But she wanted more. More kisses, more heat. And definitely more intensity. And she set out to get there.

Her fingers scraped across the velvet hardness of Castillo's shoulders, down the rock-hard curve of his biceps.

Wasn't he a big one?

With a little growl of anticipation, Lara decided to do some exploring. Reluctantly leaving those delicious lips, she nibbled her way over to that irresistible dimple, dipping her tongue in before sliding kisses along the hard angle of his jaw.

Oh, he was tasty.

She used her tongue, sliding down his stubble-roughened throat, and hummed when she reached the curve of his shoulder. It was so tempting to lean in and cuddle. But she wasn't a cuddly kind of gal, and there were definitely more interesting things to be doing.

Angling her body because she didn't want to give up

her perch over the promising bulge beneath the blanket, Lara bit the chain around his neck, tugging it aside with a jingle of metal so she could get to his sexy man nipple.

Yum.

Now this was worth waking up for, she decided.

Almost.

Something was missing.

Hot fudge?

Whipped cream?

No, that wasn't it.

It took a few seconds for the answer to penetrate her sleepy lust.

He wasn't participating.

Oh, he wasn't pushing her away or making gagging noises. His breath was coming a little faster, maybe.

But he wasn't playing.

He was staring at her.

That hard, distant military stare.

Lara blinked.

Yep, that's what he was doing.

Was that a part of their SEAL training? Have half-naked women climb all over them while they pretended to be immune and practiced their intimidating stare?

"Morning," she said after a few seconds when that stare got to her. She almost hunched her shoulders and apologized before realizing she didn't have a damned thing to be sorry for.

Hey, a girl wasn't responsible for what she did in her sleep.

"Maybe we should get up," he said after clearing his throat a couple of times.

She wanted to point out that he already appeared to be up. Quite up, *thank you very much*.

She didn't, though.

Not out of ladylike reserve. That'd be silly, since she was straddling him like a polo pony.

Nope.

She figured his dick was stabbing into her thigh hard enough that pointing it out was redundant.

She'd be damned if he'd set her aside this time.

Besides, one of his hands had slid under her sleep shirt and was now curved over her ass.

That was a clear go-ahead signal if she'd ever felt one.

"I don't think I'm done yet," she told him with a smile that was pure dare. Let him claim he didn't want her. She flexed her thighs against his hips. She'd be glad to prove him wrong.

"We really shouldn't be doing this." He sounded 100 percent sure. But his eyes were hot and his fingers were kneading her butt—whether he realized it or not.

"Why don't we discuss it?" she suggested.

"Discuss it?"

"Naked," she added, wriggling away so she could pull her nightshirt off.

He didn't let her. His hand pressed like a vise against the small of her back, the fabric locked between them.

"This is a bad idea," he muttered.

It was hard to take him seriously, though, since his fingers had worked their way under the slim fabric of her V-string and were heading south.

"Sometimes bad ideas result in really, really good sex," she whispered. Then, because she had a firm policy against chitchat before noon, Lara reached between them to grab his erection.

Oh, yeah.

It was hard.

Big and hard.

"Mmm," she hummed, licking his bottom lip.

Her eyes laughing, she met his gaze with a wiggle of her brows. He looked as if he was in pain.

Since she figured she was probably responsible for that pain, it must be her job to relieve him of it.

She gave his thick erection another squeeze. He bit back a groan. Taking advantage of his distraction, Lara shifted fast so she had the blanket out of the way and was upright and straddling him again.

Oh, baby. His dick pressed against her heat, wet delight soaking her panties.

She wanted to move. To slide up and down, in and out. To feel that long, hard length inside her, as far as he could go.

Shivering at the intensity of her desire, not sure she'd ever wanted this much, this fast, Lara ran her fingers through her hair.

She stared down at Castillo. His eyes were hot, his mouth tight. For a second, she wondered what objections he was biting back. As long as he kept them to himself, she didn't care.

Not looking away, she wrapped her fingers around the hem of her nightshirt, slowly pulling it up to reveal her skin. All of her skin. His eyes turned molten blue, his gaze so hot it could melt steel.

Lara bared her breasts and paused. She had one hell of a body and she wanted him to get a really, really good look.

Because she didn't plan on stopping for show-and-tell once she was naked.

His breath coming just a little faster, Castillo's eyes locked on her breasts and he wet his lips.

Good boy. He had the right idea.

Ready to go, Lara whipped the shirt over her head and threw it aside.

She shook her hair out of her eyes, then reached down

to cup the heavy weight of her breasts in her hands as an offering.

"Why don't we find out how many bad ideas we can come up with?" she suggested in a husky tone.

"A few dozen come to mind." He reached up, his hands covering hers.

Lara almost came then and there.

His hands were so big. So, so big and talented.

He squeezed her flesh, then shifted so he was still cupping but his fingers were free to tease her nipples.

Yum.

Lara shivered, sensations flying through her body too fast for her to identify them. All she knew was that she had never felt like this.

This wild.

This excited.

This desperate.

She arched, pressing her breasts harder into his hands. At the same time she pushed down so her clit was sliding over his dick, the fabric of her panties the only thing between them.

"More." She needed more.

"Who made you the boss?" he asked in a teasing tone.

Lara laughed.

He pinched her nipples. A zing of desire shot through her like a lightning bolt, choking her laughter.

She took a deep breath, sliding her hands over his, then down her sides. Her fingers grazed her belly button, flicking the red cherry pierced there, before moving down.

She hooked her thumbs around the narrow elastic band of her panties, then with a quick tug, ripped them off.

"Damn," he breathed, half laughing but looking pretty impressed. Until she slid her fingers lower.

His eyes followed as she angled her body up just a little so she wasn't pressed against him any longer.

She slipped her finger along her wet clitoris, her knuckle grazing his erection.

Castillo gulped.

Lara grinned.

"That's what makes me boss," she decided.

Boss.

Goddess.

Most incredibly sexy woman on earth.

Dominic was pretty sure she could lay claim to any and all of those titles.

He stared up at the gorgeous sight above him and gave fervent thanks that he was a man.

Her breasts were amazing. Large, full and heavy, tipped with rosy nipples the size of his thumb. He could spend hours worshipping her breasts alone. He wanted to bury his face between them, to slide inside that deep valley and find heaven.

Her body was a gift from Mother Nature. He had enough experience to know that there was no silicone here.

Everything about her was all natural.

All delicious.

And he was hungry.

Dominic grabbed her by the waist and lifted.

Lara squeaked, her hands grabbing as if to latch on to his shoulders, but he moved too fast. For a girl with so many curves, she was pretty light, he decided as he shifted her body up so she was straddling his chest instead of his hips.

"Sorry, boss," he said, grinning at her expression. "I always wake up hungry."

The sleepy shock left her eyes and she gave a wickedly delighted smile as she slid her finger over his mouth.

"Be my guest," she murmured, shifting her weight to her knees and leaning forward to brace her hands on the edge of the couch. *"Mangia."*

He wasn't a man who needed to be told twice.

Dominic wrapped his hands over her full butt and lifted his head. He slid his tongue along her pouting pink bud, sipping at the wet juices.

Damn.

She really was delicious.

She rose over him, panting and undulating against his thrusting tongue. Her hands gripped her breasts, fingers teasing and pulling. Desperate to take over that particular task, Dominic shifted his lips, nipping her bud between his teeth. She shuddered.

He sucked.

She exploded.

Her body clenched. Lara's fingers gripped her breasts, her head thrown back as she gave a long, keening moan so tempting, Dominic almost exploded then and there.

He called on every modicum of control, honed both from years of perfecting his sexual style and his time training in the Navy. It took every bit and more to keep from heading over the cliff when Lara shot him a heavy-lidded look and purred, then scraped her nails down his chest.

Dominic didn't remember grabbing his pants, pulling out his wallet nor putting on a condom, but long-term reflex and muscle memory assured him that he did.

Before Lara stopped shuddering, he moved. Sliding up so his back was against the couch, he grabbed Lara's hips.

"Climb on," he murmured as he yanked her down, impaling her with his rock-hard erection.

Oh, baby.

It felt like coming home.

If coming home was wrapped in sexual pleasure, layered with passion and cut with a painfully needy edge.

"Well, hello," Lara murmured in a gasping tone.

Bless her limber body, she wrapped her legs around the small of his back and angled herself so they were facing each other, her breasts at just the right height for his mouth.

"Hello," Dominic murmured, leaning forward to take one of those tasty, berry-sweet tips between his lips. He sucked hard. Lara whimpered, squirming. He didn't move his hips, though. Nope, he wanted her settled there until he was ready.

He swirled his tongue around the rock-hard tip of her breast. One hand anchored her butt to keep her where he wanted and the other cupped her breast, his fingers teasing the tip with a light strum.

Damn, she tasted good.

His dick throbbed. Need pounded through him.

But Dominic was taking his time.

Savoring.

Lara squirmed again, shifting her hips back and forth as if trying to entice him into moving, too.

Nope. Dominic knew what he liked and how he liked it.

And he was really, really liking what he had right now.

"I'm busy here," he told her, his mouth still on her breast.

"You're…" Her words cut off in a gasp when he bit, just hard enough to get her attention.

"Busy." He laved his tongue over her red bud, then blew on it, grinning when it tightened even more. She was so incredibly responsive. "Worshipping takes time, you know."

He glanced up just in time to see her eyes go soft and her lips round into an O. "You're worshipping me?"

Her tone was lightly mocking, but he could see the vulnerable sheen in her eyes.

Had no man ever shown her the adoration, the reverence she deserved?

He could tell none had. He couldn't understand why, though. Lara was gorgeous; she was funny, sweet and clever. A sassy woman with a spine of steel. And, of course, the body of a goddess.

Looked as if it was on him.

A mission he was thrilled to take, although the first he'd ever accepted while naked and straddled.

"A woman like you deserves worship," he said, his words just above a whisper as he slid his lips across her shoulder. His fingers trailed softly over her nipples, circling, swirling, brushing. He ran his hands over the silken-smooth flesh of her waist, her lush hips, down her soft thighs.

"You're beautiful," he breathed.

Lifting, he took her mouth with his. Underneath the passion was a sweetness that surprised Dominic. Her or him? The combination of the two of them? He didn't know, but he rolled with it all the same.

Her tongue slid along his, her teeth nipping as if to urge him to hurry the hell up.

Never one to disappoint a lady, he did just that.

The pace quickened. He buried his face between her breasts, his fingers working, his tongue sliding deep into the heavenly valley. His dick throbbed.

He couldn't hold out much longer.

"Dance for me," he said, his teeth tight as he resisted the urge to thrust. Hard and deep. He wanted to be inside her as deep and as far as she'd take.

But this wasn't about him.

It was about them.

Lara took over.

Her knees wedged against his thighs, she undulated. Up and down, swiveling here and there with a rhythm only she heard. But she made him feel it as she danced with his body.

Tension built, tight and needy.

Dominic gripped her thighs, his fingers dipping between to feel her wetness.

She shuddered, then shifted to welcome him into the dance.

Their eyes locked, Lara moved, slow and sensuous. Sliding up, then down his rigid cock. Wet heat gripped him, but suddenly Dominic barely felt it.

What was going on between them, the intense power in Lara's eyes—that was an even bigger turn-on.

Her fingers teased, so light they were barely there, over his shoulders, down his pecs, across his nipples, then back again.

Her breath washed over his face, just a little ragged and minty fresh.

Dominic thrust deeper, his thumb working her bud as he moved.

"Oh," Lara cried. Her eyes closed and her breath came in pants now.

He thrust harder. Faster.

She exploded.

Her orgasm was like a door opening.

Dominic's heart, his mind blew before his body even caught on that it was climax time.

His vision blurred, everything going hazy.

Except Lara's face.

Her brilliant green eyes, her pouting lip and the vision of her exploding in delight sent him over the edge.

Her body gripped him, milking every last drop of passion.

And all Dominic could think was when could they go again.

As if his orgasm pulled the plug on her energy, Lara collapsed against his chest, her face buried in the curve of his shoulder. The intimacy of their position, the implicit trust in her body, sent a warning signal so loud it burst through the passion fogging his brain.

Dominic rolled, shifting so they were both flat on the floor. Even as one arm held Lara close, emotionally he took a fifty-foot vertical shift away.

Holy hell.

Dominic was a man who appreciated sex.

He considered it one of the major reasons for living. And as a fan of life, he'd made it his mission to appreciate it as often as possible.

So he considered himself something of an expert.

An expert on good sex.

An expert on dangerous sex.

He threw one arm over his eyes, as if he could block reality along with the morning light.

If he was such a damned expert, how had he ended up here? Totally screwed.

She'd done him in.

He'd set out to show Lara what it was like to be worshipped, to give her a hot, sexy time. That's what sex was all about.

Instead, she'd blown his mind. He'd lost it.

Lost control. Lost focus.

Lost a piece of himself.

He'd never felt anything like that before.

His breath still short—a pretty rare thing for a man in his condition—he tried to calm his heart rate. *Mellow,* he thought. Bring it down. If he could convince his body this had just been another tumble, his mind would follow along, filing it under *lust-inspired oops*. A sleep-fogged mistake that could endanger the mission and totally screw with his peace of mind.

The problem was, he was reaching for her before his mind got the message. After all, if one round was bad, how much worse could two or four be?

6

LARA MADE IT a point to be honest with herself.

When she did something beyond-belief stupid, it was better to fess up and deal with it. Pretending, excuses, denial—all they did was drag out the inevitable consequences. It was like reneging on payoff to a loan shark. In the end you forked over twice as much cash, usually while crying over your broken kneecaps.

So here she was, still naked and floating on a sea of orgasmic delight, knowing she'd just made a mistake she couldn't afford to pay for.

She'd never felt anything like that.

Never lost every ounce of inhibition in her quest to make someone else feel as amazing as he made her feel.

"Hell of a way to start the morning," Castillo said, his voice husky.

With regret? With delight? She couldn't tell what was beneath the neutral surface, so she turned her head to look at him.

Yep.

Gorgeous, sexy, with sleepy eyes and that heart-melting dimple. But gorgeous or not, his expression was neutral.

Lara struggled to match it, not wanting him to know

he'd just rocked her world and blown her mind. He was already holding all the cards, so why give him any more power?

"Beats an alarm clock," she finally said in an offhand acknowledgment of his words.

His lips twitched.

Since she knew her comment hadn't been that funny, she figured he saw right through her. Lara automatically shifted to the side, tilting her chin and giving him a flirtatious look from under her lashes.

His eyes narrowed, flaming hot as his gaze skimmed the view. Good. Lara didn't like anyone looking too deep.

"I'm gonna grab a shower," he said, suddenly vaulting to his feet. *My, what a body.* Golden, smooth and muscled, he looked like something you'd see in a Greek museum. Lara's eyes shifted to his well-sculpted butt and she sighed.

She barely had time to wipe the imaginary drool off her chin when he glanced back at her.

"You wanna join me?"

Oh, boy, did she. Lara almost raised her hand for help up before the warning signals blared in her head.

"I'll wait," she said, reaching over to pull his abandoned blanket over her. "Order coffee, breakfast."

"Don't forget the bacon," he instructed on his way to the bathroom.

Life, in its infinite wisdom, had offered her a choice.

Hot guy whose tongue could make her see fireworks, in the shower. Naked and wet.

Or an unguarded door.

More than anything else, she'd wanted to climb in that shower and lick the water drops off Castillo's body. To see if he could make her standing-up-in-a-shower fantasy into a body-melting reality. To climb up and down that delicious body of his, explode into another handful of orgasms, then cuddle next to him and stare at his dimples.

So she did the only thing she could.

She ran.

Ten minutes later, Lara shifted her duffel strap more securely on her shoulder as she swayed with the moving bus, her eyes watching but not taking in passing streets.

She'd had to move fast, considering he was one of those military guys who probably showered in three minutes. The moment the bathroom door shut, she'd grabbed her bag, her laptop and backup drive. She didn't slow down to dress, instead yanking on her jeans and boots in the elevator and hiding her sleep shirt under her jacket.

The bus ground to a stop, pulling Lara from her sex-induced stupor. Shouldering her way through the people, down the steps, she gave a cursory look left and right for big goons.

Goon-free.

She rolled her eyes over Castillo's over-the-top warnings and stormed across the street. What a drama queen. King? There was definitely nothing feminine about him. His huge, um, muscles balanced out the dimples and kept him firmly on the manly side of life.

Get over it, she mentally ranted. *Quit thinking about him.* Obsessing over naked mistakes never helped.

Of course, she'd never made such a huge naked mistake before. So maybe a little obsessing was, like, an obligation.

Stopping at the top of her stairwell, Lara laid her head against the wall, barely resisting the urge to bounce it a few times. Who knew? Maybe she could shake a little sense back into her brain.

Since her body was still carrying Castillo's fingerprints, she decided to hold off beating herself up any more, at least until she'd showered. Then, if instead of heading to a friend's to crash, she was still fighting the urge to hop on a bus, ride back across town and beg him for another round? Well, there was a nice cement wall outside. She'd whack her head against that instead.

Wait. She frowned as she stomped down the empty hallway. Why was she freaking so much? Who said those guys who'd trashed her place were anything more than sloppy burglars? Castillo had probably played off the incident to get her into that hotel room. The guy was buddies with Phillip. Yet another rich frat boy out to get lucky.

Just because the fraternity was paid by the government to off bad guys didn't mean they were any different, she sniffed.

Ready to start pretending the past twelve hours hadn't happened, Lara tugged the crime scene tape off and pushed her broken door open. She'd be irritated that the super hadn't fixed it, but she wasn't sure whom the ambulance had taken away the day before.

She pulled it shut the best she could and looked around.

Her stomach slid into her toes.

She had to close her eyes, then open them again to see if maybe part of her brain had fried from sexual overload.

Nope.

It was totally trashed.

She frowned as she dropped her duffel bag next to the door then settled her fists on her hips.

It hadn't been this bad before, had it?

Had dirtbags—or her neighbors—sifted through the mess looking for valuables? Or any single item still intact?

She kicked her way to the kitchen, figuring maybe she'd open a window and let some of the ugly out. She grabbed the mail off the table, trying to remember if it had been there before.

With a drunken creak, her door swung back open.

She glanced over her shoulder, hoping it was the super with some duct tape.

Oh, shit.

No super.

No duct tape.

Lara's stomach dropped, tension slamming through her so hard she was lucky she didn't land on her ass. Her breath knotted in her chest, hurting as she tried to make her lungs work.

Looming in her doorway, looking as though he was on death's payroll, was one of the goons.

A very big, very ugly, very mean-looking goon.

"Been looking for you," he said in a heavily accented guttural growl.

Okay, so maybe Frat Boy hadn't been exaggerating about the danger thing.

She could handle this. It was broad daylight—her door didn't even shut. Her fingers shook on her hips and she felt like throwing up. But the only thing in her stomach was a grease slick of fear, so she swallowed it down and tried her only option.

Bullshit.

"You must be looking for Lara," she said, adding a strained laugh and big wide eyes. "Sorry. She's not here right now."

Mean and Ugly just stared.

Then, not even glancing around as if he might be concerned with witnesses, he stepped farther into the room.

Uh-oh.

Lara would have stepped back, but her feet were frozen to the floor.

"I'm her neighbor. She, you know, called and asked me to check her mail." She waved the envelopes as if they were covered in truth dust to verify her claim.

She couldn't tell if Mean and Ugly believed her or not. He just kept staring with those dead shark eyes.

"So, um, I can give her a message if you want."

Still nothing.

She winced, glancing past his shoulder. Was he waiting for his buddy? Didn't goons travel in pairs?

The idea of another one sent a wave of terror washing over her. Lara tried to swallow the slippery, hot fear clawing its way up her throat. She'd be okay. She was street smart; she'd handled bad before. She could handle this.

Somehow.

He moved closer.

She wanted to run. To scream. To jump up and down yelling, *no fair, dammit*.

But she couldn't move.

Lara's fingers clenched, the mail crumpling loudly. The sound snapped her out of the foggy terror. She frantically looked around for a weapon. Keys, a big stick. A stiletto.

Nothing.

She had a handful of mail.

Her bills were heavy, but she didn't figure this was gonna do more than offer up a few paper cuts.

"Look, buddy—"

Before she could finish, before she could even figure out if she was going to threaten or plead, he grabbed her arm.

Unlike when Castillo had made that very same move the night before, she didn't feel irritated with a disturbing undercurrent of turned on.

She was straight-up terrified and the only undercurrents were the kind that made her want to cry.

"Let's go."

"I don't want to go." Leaning back with all her weight—which wasn't insubstantial considering her height—she dug her heels into the carpet, the nappy fibers catching on her spiked boots. "I don't know what you want, I don't care who you are. Let go of me and get out of here or you're gonna be sorry."

Not even rolling his eyes or bothering to laugh at her empty threat, he started dragging her toward the door.

Lara didn't make it easy.

She struggled, kicking at his legs, trying to get close enough to scratch his face. She briefly considered biting, but didn't figure he'd had his rabies shot.

Nothing worked.

She screamed. So loud and hard it felt as if the scream scoured her throat raw.

When nobody appeared, she screamed again.

And kicked him, driving the pointy toe of her boot into the fleshy part of his calf.

He didn't even slow.

Holy shit.

Terror grabbed tight, her heart racing so fast the blood almost burst out of her ears, Lara tried to catch her breath. Tried to restart her brain.

Nothing.

He was a foot from the door.

No.

No way in hell this ugly guy was hauling her off.

Fueled by the hideous images of what he might do, Lara launched herself at the guy. She wrapped her arms around his neck, her legs around his side so her heels dug into his arm. Clinging to him like a sideways burr, she ignored the disease potential and chomped her teeth into his shoulder with a vicious growl.

He grunted.

And let go of her arm.

Lara had just enough forethought to know if she let go, he would win. Instead, she hitched herself onto his back, beating his ear with one hand and yanking his greasy hair with the other.

"You're gonna want to release her now."

Lara heard the warning over the goon's cussing and her own pants. She quit struggling, her body sagging on the goon's back as her gaze flew to the doorway.

Castillo.

Her hero.

Tears filled her eyes, her breath coming in gasps as she tried to take it in.

She was safe.

No matter what happened now, she was safe.

Castillo would take care of her.

"Lara." That's all he said. Her name, in that unemotional I'm-a-military-machine voice.

She'd never heard anything so wonderful.

Knowing what he wanted as if he were holding up cue cards, she let go, then jumped rather than slid off the goon's back. And promptly landed on her ass at the rapid descent. She winced, both at the jarring impact and at the humiliatingly lame move.

"I'm here for the woman. You can go."

"Yeah?" Castillo's military mask cracked enough for his grin to escape. Then he shook his head. "And if I don't want to go?"

Lara didn't want to hear the guy's response. At least, not while she was flat on her ass on the floor. She shifted, trying to stay out of the goon's line of sight as she got to her feet.

Apparently he had eyes in the back of his head, because he didn't even look around as he swung his hand.

She moved fast, so instead of sending her back to the floor the blow only grazed her face.

"Lara!" Castillo snapped.

She ran toward him at the same time he launched himself into the air, bending at the waist so his feet slammed into the guy's chest.

Lara gaped.

Sprawled on the floor, the goon glared as he reached into the pocket of his jacket. Before he could bring his hand out, Castillo rolled from the floor into a crouch and waved his fingers in a bring-it-on motion.

The guy slowly lowered his hand.

"I told you you'd be sorry," she taunted, wiping the blood from her lip with the back of her wrist.

It was a lot easier to sound cocky here, standing behind her very own SEAL.

Castillo shook his head at her, then jerked his head to indicate she should move to the door.

Lara bent down to grab her duffel. Before she could straighten, the goon gave a roar. He surged to his feet, grabbing a chair—the only intact piece of furniture in the room—and swung it at Castillo's head.

Castillo didn't even flinch as the wood splintered over the arm he'd raised to protect his skull. Instead, he reached out and grabbed the guy by the neck, then lifted him off his feet.

In a blink the guy had a knife in his hand.

Screaming, Lara swung her duffel at the guy at the same time Castillo grabbed the guy's hand. He might have planned a few other moves, but Lara kept swinging her duffel and getting in the way. She didn't care. Fury filled her like nothing she'd ever felt in her life.

Castillo had saved her and this creepy guy wanted to cut him? No way. No way in hell.

"Lara." Castillo growled her name a third time.

Panting, her hair poking her in the eyes and her lip

throbbing, Lara clutched the duffel in her arms for a second, then ran to the door.

Her back was only turned to the men for maybe two seconds. But when she reached the door and looked back, the goon was lying on the floor.

"Is he dead?" she gasped.

He looked dead.

"Move."

Lara nodded, but she couldn't take her eyes off the crumpled body on the floor.

"Now."

Lara blinked, swallowing hard against the nasty taste in her mouth. She wet her lips, looked at the man, then at Castillo.

He wasn't even winded.

If he'd had more than a half an inch of hair, she didn't think it'd be out of place. Nope, he looked totally—what was that term he liked?

Copacetic.

He didn't even hurry out the door. He just sort of sauntered, grabbing her around the waist as he went and hauling her along.

Lara wanted to run, but Castillo kept their pace mellow. Through the hall, down the stairs, out of the building. He paused at the bottom of the stairs, scanning the street.

Lara followed his gaze, her body feeling like a rubber band stretched too tight. She knew she'd snap at any second and hoped like hell the goon didn't have friends out here. She wasn't sure she could take more.

The coast must have been clear, though, because Castillo headed for the Harley parked in front of the building.

He didn't let go of her until they reached it, then after giving her a look that warned against trying to run, he unlocked the saddlebag and pulled out a helmet. Without a word, he handed it to her.

He grabbed another one off the handlebar. How it hadn't been stolen was a mystery to Lara. Maybe he had some kind of badass force field around the motorcycle.

"I'm sorry," Lara murmured, looking at the bruises on his face. She twined her fingers around the helmet strap to keep them from reaching up to touch, soothe the skin over his cheekbone. That was her fault. She wasn't the one who'd broken the chair over his face, but it was still her fault.

From the chilly look in his blue eyes, Castillo would agree. Not wanting to hear that look put into words, Lara awkwardly tucked her duffel under her arm, then bent to pull the helmet on. It didn't have a visor, so the view of Castillo's stare was clear and bright.

Lovely.

"How am I supposed to hold on to my stuff?" She held out the duffel she'd clung to like a teddy bear, showing him the broken straps.

His eyes narrowed and for a second she thought he'd tell her where she could put her stuff. Then he lifted her duffel by the edge, both straps dangling loose. With one hand, he flipped open the leather saddlebag again. He glanced at the duffel, then at the size of his bag. It wasn't going to fit.

She chewed on her thumbnail, waiting to see what he was going to do.

His sigh was a work of art. The kind of sound that said a million long-suffering things meant to inspire all sorts of guilt. It worked. She was ready to tell him she didn't need all of it, just her laptop, when he snapped the duffel open with a tug of his hands.

She cringed.

He dumped the contents into the saddlebag, reaching

over the bike to stuff her laptop into the one on the other side with his clothes. Then he tossed the ripped bag into a nearby trash can. Not once did he meet her eyes.

She was glad. She remembered the cold fury in his gaze when they'd left the apartment. She'd rather not see it aimed her way.

Still, furious or not, he'd saved her.

And he'd saved her stuff.

She wanted to ask if that guy was dead. She wanted to apologize for running. For putting herself in danger and him in the position of having to play hero.

"Thank you," she whispered instead.

He gave a jerk of his shoulder, handed her a pair of sunglasses, then nodded to the Harley.

"Climb on."

It was probably a bad time to joke that the last time he'd said that to her, they'd both been naked.

She had a feeling this round wasn't going to feel nearly as good, nor have nearly as fun an ending.

DOMINIC RODE AUTOMATICALLY, his eyes on the road and his mind focused on their destination. A part of his brain acknowledged the woman whose arms were wrapped around his waist, whose thighs were pressed against the backs of his. But he told himself he was only aware enough to know she was still on the bike.

She'd walked out on him.

So it wasn't hard to believe she'd leap off the back of a moving Harley. At least, his ego didn't think so.

He gripped the handlebars tight to force himself not to speed up. To race the bike as fast as he could away from one simple, horrifying truth.

Lara had had sex with him.

Incredible, body-shaking, multiorgasmic sex.

Twice.

And she'd walked out.

No, given that she was still wearing the sleep shirt she'd stripped off her body and left behind not so much as an eyelash, she hadn't walked out.

She'd run out.

On him.

He simply couldn't comprehend it.

Destination, he told himself, flexing his fingers on the grips again.

Just focus on where we're going. Deal with the rest later.

Donner Lake caught his eye, the brilliant blue sparkling as the sun hit high overhead. An hour down, three to go.

Then he could shake Lara off his back, get a little distance, check in with the team. And beat the hell out of some useless, inanimate object. Just for fun.

She'd freaking run out on him.

Him.

He wasn't an idiot. He knew that kind of thing happened. Just not to him.

He was there to protect her. She had seen firsthand the danger she was in. Yet she'd run—not walked—away. She'd stupidly risked her life and endangered the mission.

Fine.

From this second forward, she wasn't female, she wasn't sexy, she wasn't his every fantasy come true.

She was a mission.

Duty.

Nothing else.

Dammit.

LARA WONDERED HOW long a person could clench their teeth before their jaw exploded. She didn't need to see Castillo's face to know he was still clenching. Even his shoulder blades were tight. She could almost hear his molars grinding through their helmets.

Okay, so she shouldn't have blown off his warnings. She should have waited, let him play bodyguard. She shouldn't have run from the hotel like a hooker with his wallet buried in her bra. She shouldn't have given in to lust and had sex with him. Not the first or second time.

Hell, she shouldn't have gotten out of bed that morning.

It was all her fault.

Her fault he was hurt.

Her fault he'd had to, maybe, kill that guy.

Her fault for all the trouble he was going to be in.

Did SEALs get in trouble for things like that?

He hadn't acted as if he was worried.

Nope.

He'd been an unemotional military machine.

Except for the flash of fury she'd seen in his eyes before he'd turned away.

No wonder.

She'd used him.

Sure, she could excuse her morning swan dive onto his body as a sleep-induced mistake. But she'd known what she was doing when he'd gone down on her. She'd been totally aware of what she had in her body when she came.

She'd used the poor man for her own selfish pleasures.

Over and over again.

He'd made it clear she was a duty. His mission.

And she'd sneaked up and seduced him.

No wonder he was so pissed.

Even knowing she was pushing her luck, Lara couldn't help but give in to the emotional exhaustion beating down on her and leaned her head against Castillo's leather-clad back. Her body automatically followed, pressing tight against his warmth.

She owed him. She didn't know how or with what she'd pay him back. Since all the ideas that came to mind involved his body being naked, she figured she'd better keep thinking on it.

SERIOUSLY?

How the hell was he supposed to pretend she was nothing more than an assignment when she pressed those luxuriously delicious breasts against his chest?

He knew she wasn't wearing a bra. That the only things between his bare back and her rosy nipples were a couple layers of fabric.

He should have stopped and bought her a leather jacket. Except that'd require talking, and he wasn't ready to talk to the woman who'd run out, almost getting herself cut to ribbons and made into some goon's plaything.

If she'd compromised the mission, Dominic would have failed. If Valdero's creep had grabbed her, the team's shot at getting Banks out would be a helluva lot harder.

By taking the guy down, Castillo had alerted the drug lord that the team had made him. He'd take steps to counter them.

Before leaving Reno, Castillo had sent Brody a coded text.

So now the team knew that Castillo had let a woman slip through his fingers. He'd say Banks would have a heyday with that, but the guy wasn't friendly enough to give anyone a bad time. He was, though, as Dominic's superior, in a position to make his life hell for not keeping Lara safe.

Now, instead of lying low and playing chill in Reno, he was taking his mission—that's all she was now, dammit—

to the base, where he could access resources to counter Valdero's next move.

That'd mean explanations.

Of why he was there instead of on leave.

Of why he had Banks's sister in tow.

And why he knew about a top-secret mission that was still in play.

Dominic growled into the wind, then realized he'd been squeezing the grips so hard they were flying twenty miles an hour over the posted limit.

He reluctantly throttled back.

Yeah. No question about it. Lara had put the mission in jeopardy.

And she'd walked out on him.

7

LARA WASN'T STUPID enough to fall asleep on the back of a motorcycle. But she'd definitely been in a daze for the past hour. Until the bike slowed, pulling off the freeway.

Her head still lying against Castillo's back, she opened her eyes, the dark glasses shielding the sun as it reflected off rows and rows of grapevines.

Wine country?

Good.

She could use a good drink.

So, other than Northern California, where were they?

And why?

Her stomach growled, hunger overpowering the fluttering nerves that'd taken up residence there.

What was he going to do with her?

She wasn't afraid he'd hurt her. But he might dump her on someone else. Someone who wouldn't be as good at keeping her safe. Lara wasn't proud of the fact, but she knew if it came down to that, she just might beg.

No.

She was his assignment. He'd said so.

Which meant he'd keep her safe until he was unassigned.

Trying to believe, hoping like crazy it was true, she flexed her fingers on the leather around Castillo's waist and tried to relax.

She almost found her daze again as the bike meandered along back roads between forests, fields and vineyards. Did he think someone was following them? Or was wherever he was going really in the middle of nowhere?

She still wasn't sure when he turned onto a dirt path marked by two huge redwoods, throttling the Harley back to a dull roar.

He wove down a path so narrow a car wouldn't fit. Sun winked between tall trees, the tires kicking up pine needles and the exhaust ruffling the bushes.

It'd be a great place to bury a body.

Lara seriously hoped she hadn't pissed him off that much.

Then he came to a clearing.

Her nerves dissipated.

Her mouth dropped.

It was like being suffused with a hefty shot of mellow. Every muscle relaxed and Lara smiled.

There, at the far end of the clearing, was the cutest cabin. So darling she expected a little girl in a red cape to come skipping through the trees.

Castillo stopped, turned off the motor. He gave a jerk of his shoulders. She let go of his waist and leaned back far enough that plenty of air fit between their bodies. He didn't have to shake her off twice, she sniffed.

He pulled his phone out, angling it so she couldn't see what he was doing. As if she was so nosy she'd try and read over his shoulder? Lara rolled her eyes, wondering if he'd gotten any medals for his paranoia.

Then she wrinkled her nose, remembering that he'd been spot-on with his last *paranoid* warning. She looked toward the trees so she wouldn't catch sight of what he was doing. Just in case.

Eventually—one, two, twenty minutes or so later—he tucked the phone into his pocket. He kicked the stand down, then swung his leg over the seat to dismount the bike. Big, sturdy thing that it was, it only shifted a little with Lara still perched on the back.

He pulled something else out of his pocket.

A cool military device? Some kind of homing signal that'd open a secret cave in the trees?

When he aimed it at the cabin, she saw a small red light above the door go out.

Security system?

Okay, it was still cool.

She glanced at Castillo to comment, then caught her breath.

He was unzipping his jacket, the black leather parting. Oh, yeah, she sighed, noting that his shirt was a lot tighter today. The soft cotton of his tee molded a chest that was as delicious as it was hard. Lara licked her lips, her eyes skimming over his flat belly. She wished the shirt was tight there, too, because he had abs worth worshipping.

She really hadn't spent enough time appreciating them while he was naked. She should have kissed her way over that chest, spent a good bit of time with the abs on her way down. But she'd been in too much of a hurry to get to the good stuff.

Story of her life.

Lara forced herself to look away before she started drooling. She glanced at her watch, noting that it'd been four hours since he'd even looked at her. That jerk of his shoulders was the only indication since they'd left her apartment building that he knew she was there.

It was enough to make a girl forget she was sorry and make a play—a very naughty play—for his attention.

He'd saved her, she reminded herself.

Jumping his body and using him for wild sex was a poor thank-you.

Maybe.

"Where are we?" she finally asked.

"We're not driving to Coronado on a bike," was all he said.

Lara looked around for an alternate form of transportation.

But unless that darling cabin flew or he had a transporter in the trees somewhere, there was nothing.

He didn't elaborate, just strode toward the cabin and climbed the steps.

Afraid it'd fall over without his presence, Lara climbed off the bike. She was glad he'd gone inside, since her dismount wasn't nearly as graceful as his.

Lara stood next to the bike, looking around while she tried to decide what to do. He hadn't invited her into the cabin, but he hadn't warned her to stay out, either.

A loud rustling broke the peaceful silence, the bushes shaking off to the right.

Rude or not, Lara wasn't staying out here. Her fingers fumbled with the buckle on the saddlebag, her heart racing as she tried to get it open. Finally, she threw the leather flap over, grabbed her laptop and, almost tripping over her own feet, ran toward the cabin.

She made it up the three wide plank steps without a problem, but her toe hit the seam on the porch, sending her flying through the open door.

She caught her balance just before her knees hit the floor.

Righting, her laptop cradled against her chest, she blew her hair out of her eyes and grimaced at Castillo.

"Sorry. I'm usually more graceful," she muttered.

Blushing—something she hadn't done since her teens—Lara avoided his gaze, glancing around instead.

Wow.

This wasn't anything like what she imagined Red's grandma's cabin looked like.

One huge room with a couple of doors jutting off at the back, it was *Field & Stream* meets *Modern Life.* Slick, clean lines, leather furniture and a TV that took up an entire wall. She'd call it man land, but there were no pinups on the walls or dirty socks on the floor.

"Where are we?" she asked for the second time.

And, of course, for the second time Castillo ignored her.

She forced herself to look at him and realized she shouldn't have been embarrassed. He probably hadn't even seen her almost face-plant at his feet. Obviously, in his mind she still didn't exist.

Seriously?

How long was he going to keep this up?

All because—what? She'd left before round two of the hot sweaty delight match? Or because she hadn't cowered under the hotel bed, whimpering for him to keep her safe?

It was stupid. What was done was done, no harm, no foul—well, except to the questionable body back in her apartment.

But, still…

"You are such a girl," she snapped.

Feeling as though the roller coaster of a day had finally derailed, Lara stomped into what was clearly the living area, threw herself on the couch and, laptop still cradled close, glared at Castillo.

"I'm a what?" At least he was looking at her again, even if his expression did hint toward worries about her sanity.

"A girl." Lara carefully tucked her laptop onto the cushion next to her so she could throw her hands in the air. "Your feelings get hurt. Instead of talking about it, or even bitching about it, you go into deep chill. The cold shoulder. The silent treatment."

His eyes iced over. Whether her words pissed him off more or he was just affirming her claim, she couldn't tell. Because he *still* didn't say a damned thing.

Lara's hands fisted, her teeth tight to hold back a frustrated scream.

"See," she ground out. "A girl."

He gave a dismissive shake of his head. Then went right back to pretending she didn't exist while he thumbed through the stack of mail on the counter.

It was enough to make a woman want to strip bare again just to prove she could get a rise out of the guy.

Lara was too exhausted, though.

As if that thought was permission to let go, her entire body seemed to sag into itself. Her shoulders fell and her chin drooped. Her fingers were so heavy, all she could do was drop her hands to her lap.

But when Castillo stepped into the room, she snapped to attention.

"You can take a shower, get some rest. Bathroom and bed are through there." He gestured to the door on the left. "We leave in the morning."

"Where are we going?"

She might as well have asked where they were again, since the response was exactly the same.

Nothing.

Instead, he grabbed a paper bag from the kitchen,

walked out the door. Lara shifted her aching body off the couch to follow, but before she got to the door he was back.

"Your stuff." He shoved the bag into her arms.

Her stuff.

Nice.

Her entire world was now contained in a brown paper bag.

Life was good at whipping out those little ironies.

Ready to cry, Lara carried the bag to the couch to set it next to her laptop.

"Get some rest. I'll be back later with food."

"What? Wait." Lara hurried back across the room. She grabbed his arm. The rock-hard muscles were a tempting distraction, but she managed to resist the urge to pet him. "You can't leave me here alone."

"Sure, I can. I leave. You stay. Easy."

Easy? Then why was she seeing black spots dancing in front of her eyes?

"But what if those guys come? More of them?"

"They won't." At her panicked look, he waved his free hand in a circle to indicate the cabin. "The space is secure. You'll be fine."

No, she wouldn't. Not without him. Lara wet her lips, her racing heart barely keeping up with her spinning thoughts.

"But I'm hungry. I didn't get breakfast, remember?"

His eyes chilled.

Oops. She winced.

That probably wasn't the best thing to remind him of.

He pulled his arm away.

"There are crackers, dry cereal, that kind of thing in the kitchen."

Lara swallowed hard, trying to keep from begging. She

knew it wouldn't do any good and she figured she'd humiliated herself enough for one day. For one lifetime, even.

She grabbed her last option: bravado.

"You really think I'll stick around if you leave? C'mon, we've already seen how that works, haven't we?" She made sure her smile was both cocky and seductive, then tiptoed teasing fingers up his arm. "It won't be nearly as easy to find me out there with all those trees, you know."

He smirked.

"You do know the California mascot is the bear, right?"

With that, he grabbed the stack of mail, turned heel and walked out the front door.

Lara didn't even have time to yank her chin off her chest and ask where he was going before he slammed it shut. The slick sound of a lock sliding home rang out, followed by the roar of his bike.

She ran to the window in time to see him ride away.

Lara beat her fist against the glass, both comforted and infuriated that it was as solid as steel.

She sniffed as her gaze drifted to the dense woods visible outside the cabin.

Locks could keep bears out, right?

"YOU GET THE timing on the truck looked at?" Dominic asked, striding across his mother's kitchen to grab a beer to go with his lunch. "I told you it was off last time I was home."

"Yeah, yeah. You told me, I got it fixed." Lucas rolled his eyes. "You ever get tired of telling people what to do? As bossy as you are, I'm surprised you're not a captain yet."

"Give me time." Dominic grinned. Captain Castillo. Yeah, that had a nice ring to it. "I'm not bossy. I'm wise, big brother. Wisdom is meant to be shared. Especially when your ass is gonna be stranded on the side of the road without it."

"Yeah, yeah. So why's your wise ass back here? I thought you'd been called to duty."

"Not officially." Dominic wasn't saying more than that. He'd been cleared to bring his brother in as far as using Castillo Security to track Banks's sister. But that was the extent of it.

"You had me run someone. The sister of one of your team, right? You get her taken care of?"

Oh, yeah, he'd taken real good care of her.

He'd scared the hell out of her, stalked her to her apartment, done her on a hotel room floor, intimidated her, then locked her in his cabin.

Of course, she'd doubted his word, blown his mind, sexed him stupid, then walked out on him.

All in the space of twenty-four hours.

They were one hell of a couple.

"Dom?" Lucas prodded.

He gave a jerk of his chin, hoping Lucas would take it for a nod.

"So you're off duty again?"

"Not yet."

Lucas dropped into the opposite chair and gave him a narrow look.

"Where's the girl?"

Dominic debated. Technically, his association with Lara wasn't classified. It wasn't even sanctioned. So Lucas knowing wasn't a big deal.

But it felt like one.

Finally, Dominic sighed and admitted, "My place."

"What?" Lucas yelped. "You brought her here?"

If he'd accused his brother of dressing in drag and joining a nunnery, Lucas couldn't have sounded more surprised.

"It's a long drive to Coronado," was all Dominic said, focusing on his lunch.

"But…you brought her back here?"

Dominic grimaced.

He didn't know why his brother kept asking that question with such a shocked expression. It wasn't as if he hadn't brought women back to his place before. That was one of the key reasons he had the cabin on the far side of the Castillo property instead of a room here at the main house.

To bring women.

He looked up from his plate, heaped high with tamales, beans and rice, and shrugged.

"Yeah. She's locked up in my cabin."

"Seriously?" Lucas scratched his head. "Is she a hostage or something?"

"She's an assignment with a history of stupidity." Like showing him new levels of sexual pleasure, then running out on him before he could see how much better it could get. "She's not safe on her own."

"So why didn't you bring her to the house for lunch?"

A late lunch, since the rest of the family and the ranch hands had eaten and, even though it was Saturday, were already back to work. But all it'd taken was putting on his sad face to get his grandmother to heat up a plate before she'd left for her place. He'd fill another for Lara before he went back to the cabin. See? Nice guy.

"I told you, she's an assignment." Dominic hunched over his plate, trying not to feel guilty over leaving Lara there. Alone. He remembered her face, pale with exhaustion and pinched with fear.

Damn.

Apparently rejection made him a class-A jerk.

So much for being a nice guy with a talent for charming the ladies.

"If she's just a job, why're you hiding her away?" Lucas asked, obviously trying to push his little brother's buttons. "Your usual MO is to keep women away from the house because you say they're temporary and you don't want them getting any crazy long-term ideas. So what's the deal? Is this assignment of yours gonna take one look at your graduation picture in the hallway and start hinting at ring sizes?"

Dominic poured more mole over his tamale, cut a bite, then stared at his fork. *Dammit.*

Why was he keeping Lara locked up?

For her safety? Clearly not, since she'd be safer with him. They'd already proved that point.

Because having her tucked away would keep temptation at bay? As if he wasn't imagining what she'd taste like naked, covered in mole sauce, with every bite he took?

Because he didn't want her to know anything about his family? How fair was that, given that he knew damn near everything about hers?

Dominic frowned.

"I'll bring her back for dinner," he finally conceded.

"Whoa," Lucas said, holding up a hand. "Dinner? You sure?"

Dominic rolled his eyes.

"You were just giving me shit for not bringing her to the house, now you're putting up caution over her coming to dinner. What's your problem?"

"Coming to the house, lunch in the kitchen, that's casual. Dinner is the whole family, sitting down telling stories. You know Matteo is gonna do everything he can to make you look bad."

Lara could probably match their little brother story for story on that topic.

"So?" Dominic shrugged. "Celia will defend me with stories about how awesome I am."

He knew which of his siblings Lara was likely to believe, though. Dominic shoved his plate away, food barely touched. It wasn't his looks or amazing sexual prowess that made women love him. Sure, those probably factored in, but he knew it had more to do with the simple fact that he wasn't a jerk. He respected women. Respected their choices.

Except he hadn't respected Lara's.

Instead, he'd let his bruised ego have a poutfest, leaving a scared, terrorized woman starving back at his cabin.

"I gotta go," he said, heading for the door.

"You're really bringing her back for dinner?" Lucas asked, pulling the plate toward him to finish what Dominic hadn't.

Crap. Food. He needed to feed her something before dinner.

Dominic opened the fridge, pulling out containers of leftovers and stacking them on the wide granite countertop. He grabbed a bag from under the sink and, not bothering to plate the food, slid all the containers inside.

There. She'd have plenty to choose from before they took off in the morning.

"I need your truck tomorrow," he told his brother as he gathered the food and headed for the door again.

"Sure. I need it in the evening, though," Lucas said around a mouthful of tamale.

"Gonna be tough. I'm taking it down to Coronado."

Dominic didn't wait to hear his brother's protests.

He jammed the food in his saddlebag and headed back to the cabin. This route was a lot more direct than the one he'd taken a couple hours ago. But he'd been trying to hide his location.

Not from Valdero's goons.

From Lara.

Could he be a bigger jerk?

Repentant and ready to make amends, he unlocked the cabin a few minutes later, calling Lara's name.

Nothing.

He set the bag on the kitchen counter before striding to the closed guest room door. He tapped lightly in case she was asleep, then eased the door open.

"Lara?"

She wasn't in bed.

She wasn't in the bathroom.

Dominic returned to the living room, noting that her stuff was missing.

Damn.

He growled, frustrating surging through him.

Had she braved the bears?

Knowing it was entirely his fault, furious that his ego had gotten in the way of his duty—and of keeping Lara safe—Dominic cussed.

Trained to check and double-check, even though he was sure there was nothing to be found, he pushed open his own bedroom door.

Nada.

Before he could cuss again, Lara walked out of his bathroom.

Nude.

Blessedly nude and wet, surrounded by a cloud of steam.

"Damn," Dominic breathed.

Rock hard and ready to roll, his dick echoed the sentiment.

She was like something out of a dream.

Or his hottest fantasy.

Gorgeous from the white terry cloth wrapped around her hair like a crown to the tips of her polished red toenails, she screamed sex appeal.

Sex appeal waiting in his bedroom.

Covered in water.

Dominic shoved his hands in his pockets, hoping the extra pressure would keep his erection at bay.

"Oops." Looking as surprised as he, although a lot more horrified, Lara dragged the towel from her hair to wrap around her body. "I, um, I didn't hear you come in."

Voiceless, the image of her naked perfection still imprinted on his brain, Dominic could only nod.

He was a man who relished serving, who took pride in his career and worked damned hard to be the best he could. But sometimes it got ugly. It got dirty, depressing and disheartening.

When it got rough, lying on a cot in a tent in the desert or in an aircraft carrier berth on his way to a dangerous mission, Dominic slid into fantasyland. The fantasies were as varied as there were women. But one in particular always made its way through his mind: he fantasized about coming home to clear his head of the ugliness, to find peace. In his fantasy, he walked into his bedroom to find his fantasy woman. Naked, nubile and willing. Ready to make him forget, to heal his soul.

He'd never put a face to the fantasy.

But looking at Lara, he knew he'd never have it again without seeing her.

"Um, the other shower didn't have shampoo," she said, wetting her lips.

Dominic almost groaned.

Sex with Lara once could be called a mistake.

A bad judgment call.

He was a man who prided himself in knowing the right thing to do. For himself, for others.

The right thing, right now, would be to apologize, turn around and get the hell out of the room.

He knew it.

If this was anyone else, he'd be smacking him upside the head and telling him to move his ass before he stepped into FUBAR land.

But this wasn't anyone else.

It was him.

And it was Lara.

His fantasy woman.

8

Oh, boy.

Lara was grateful that whoever owned this cabin had splurged on ultraplush towels. Because the terry cloth and her fingers were the only thing hiding her nipples' instantaneous reaction to the look in Castillo's eyes.

She'd figured he'd be gone longer.

She'd scarfed down a couple of handfuls of Cheerios, explored the place from end to end to make sure there was no evidence that bears had entered. Then she'd realized she was exhausted. Unwilling to collapse without a shower, she'd picked the bigger one for no other reason than it felt good.

"I didn't expect you back this soon," she told him, wishing he'd quit staring like that. If he didn't, she was seriously afraid she'd be tossing the towel aside and jumping his body in fifteen seconds. She noted the heat in his blue gaze and swallowed. Maybe fewer than fifteen.

"I felt bad about leaving you here," he finally said. His words were husky as he stepped farther into the room. He stopped next to the bed. A huge mattress covered in ocean-blue silk, it suddenly seemed like a glowing beacon screaming *jump on and ride.*

Castillo shrugged out of his coat, letting the leather drop to the floor without a glance.

Lara almost took a step back, then automatically stopped. She knew better than showing any sign of weakness. But all she could think of was how good it had been. Had it only been that morning? It seemed like forever—and ten seconds ago—that he'd made her explode with pleasure.

Her body craved more.

Her mind warned against it.

Lara was torn.

Castillo stepped closer.

"Sex is a bad idea," she murmured.

"Then let's be bad," he said with a husky laugh, tossing the challenge she'd issued the last time back in her face. Then, upping the game, he added, "I'll make bad so good for you."

Oh.

She melted.

Her resistance.

Her reluctance.

Her thighs.

They all turned to mush at the look in his blue eyes.

Good or not, Lara knew they shouldn't.

Anything done once could be written off as a mistake. Oopsie.

Twice?

That was flipping life's warning system the bird.

That meant when the repercussions hit—and they would—the no-whining allowed rule was in effect. She'd have to graciously accept whatever paybacks she was dealt.

She watched Dominic's fingers move over the buttons of his shirt, each one revealing a little more of that silky golden skin.

Her throat was so dry she had to swallow twice to wet it. She couldn't remember any of the logical reasons to hold on to her towel. She knew there were some—probably great ones.

She wet her lips and took a deep breath as Castillo dropped his shirt to the floor.

Okay, fine.

Life, gracious acceptance was in effect.

With that promise, Lara did the only thing she could.

She dropped her towel, spread her arms and said, "Let's go, big boy."

Anticipation swirled, heat danced over Lara's skin as Castillo held up one hand, keeping her from moving until he'd looked his fill.

His eyes were fire as they skimmed from the top of her wet hair, over her bare face and down.

Down, down, down.

Her nipples beaded.

Hot moisture pooled between her thighs.

It was as if her body was on fire.

Hot, flaming tongues of desire licked over her skin.

And he hadn't even touched her yet.

"You're so gorgeous," he murmured, stepping closer.

Close enough that she could feel the heat radiating off his body.

Close enough that she could reach out and touch.

Since she'd accepted that she'd be paying a price, and acknowledged that she'd accept it, whatever it was, Lara wanted to relish every drop of pleasure this affair had to offer for as long as it lasted.

"You know what we missed last time," she mused, sliding her fingers over his chest. So hard, yet so soft. She followed the dusting of black hair down to his waistband, then tucked her fingers behind his zipper and tugged him closer.

"I thought we did a pretty good job this morning," he told her as his hands tunneled into her hair, tangling in the wet strands as he cupped the back of her head to tilt her up to meet his mouth.

Looking into his laughing eyes, Lara pretended to consider that. Just before his lips touched hers, she pressed her hand flat against his chest to stop him.

"You could say it was pretty good," she agreed softly, tracing his bottom lip with her tongue. "But is good good enough?"

"You want to do better?"

"Great? Amazing? Awesome, perhaps?"

"How about mind-blowing?" he asked before he took her mouth.

Then he proceeded to do just that…blow her mind.

Lara didn't know who moved when, or how his pants or boots disappeared.

All she knew was that his hands never left her body, his mouth never slowed on its quest of pleasure.

His body slid over hers, hard and naked. Lara shivered at the contrast between them. She wanted to touch, to feel, to drive him as crazy as he was driving her.

With that in mind, she shifted, trying to reverse their positions.

"My turn to call the shots," Castillo said, grabbing her arms and dragging them over her head. While he bracketed them in one hand, Lara arched so her breasts teased his chest, hoping the temptation would hurry his shots along.

"What've you got in mind?" she asked as he shifted on the mattress so he was sitting upright, her hands still captive.

He didn't answer. Instead, he cast a quick glance around the room, then leaned over to open the bedside table drawer. Grinning, he pulled out a length of rope.

"You keep rope by your bed?" Lara frowned at him. "Why do you keep rope by your bed?"

"I was practicing knots." He held up the length of soft-looking white rope, knots every few inches, as evidence. "Sailor knots. It's how I get to sleep at night."

"Right," she said with a laugh. She tugged her hand, wanting to toss the rope aside so they could get back to the fun.

He didn't let go.

Instead, he shifted to wrap the rope around one of the spindles of his headboard.

"Oh, no, I don't think so." Lara shook her head so fast her hair slapped her across the cheeks. "You want some passive pushover, you've got the wrong girl. You can't get it on without the bondage kink, then you should look for someone else."

"You have control issues," he teased, wrapping the rope around one wrist, then the other. The fibers were soft, like the silk bedspread at her back. But she was still at his mercy.

Lara scowled, looking for anger to throw at him.

But she was so excited that if there was any, it was buried beneath the lust surging through her. She'd never had any submissive fantasies, but there was something insanely sexy about the way Castillo was looking at her: as though he was contemplating all the delicious things he could do to her body while she just lay back and enjoyed.

"I didn't agree to this," she started to say. Before she could come up with a stronger argument, he leaned down to suck her nipple into his mouth.

Hot and wet.

Oh, God.

Desire shot through her, nipple to wet lips, making her quiver.

His hands skimmed, his tongue swirled.

Castillo used her body like his favorite plaything. He kneaded her breasts, his teeth nipping before he angled lower, his tongue sipping her juices while his fingers worked her aching flesh.

Lara's fingers wrapped tight around the headboard spindle, her back arching and her heels digging into the mattress.

Her breath came in pants, her chest on fire and her body covered in a light sheen of sweat.

His tongue was magic, but it wasn't enough.

Not even close.

"More," she demanded between moans.

Under heavy lids, she watched Castillo sheathe himself with a condom he must have grabbed along with the rope.

Heart pounding, she wet her lips as he slid his palms up the insides of her thighs, spreading her legs to make room for him.

His eyes locked on hers as he slid inside.

Her body took him in, her mind blank to everything except the exquisite pleasure.

Slowly, so deliciously slowly, he pressed deeper.

Then he slid out.

In and out.

Plunging.

Harder. Faster.

Lara's body tightened; desire coiled tight.

His eyes still holding hers prisoner, he grinned.

A wickedly gorgeous smile.

As she went over, a warning bell chimed loud enough to be heard through her screams of pleasure.

He was an addiction.

A temptation.

A heartbreaking adoration that she didn't think she'd ever recover from.

But as the waves of pleasure pounded through her body, Lara simply couldn't care. Her arms still tied overhead, she gave herself to him completely.

Right here, right now, he could have her.

Her attention.

Her body.

And yes, her heart.

He thrust again, this time anchoring her hips higher so his thrust drove so deep, Lara couldn't help it. She came again.

And again and again and again.

PLEASURE-FILLED HOURS LATER, Lara curled into her lover's arms, her body still purring while her mind floated from offhand thought to random observation.

The man had the most amazing tongue. It should be registered a lethal sex weapon.

And his skin was so smooth. Like raw silk over concrete. She sighed as her fingers skimmed his bicep. So big.

This was probably a mistake, she acknowledged as she slid the arch of her foot up and down his hair-roughened calf. But her body felt so good. *She* felt so good.

Since feeling this good, this content, was a new thing, was it so bad to spend a little time experiencing it? It wasn't as if she was crazy enough to think there was more between them than incredible sex and their questionable connection to her brother.

She didn't even know his first name. Nobody got all mushy over a guy when she didn't even know what to call him. Clearly this was just sex. Wild, hot, mind-blowing sex.

Nothing to worry about.

Lara worried her bottom lip for a second, then, unable to stop herself, asked, "What's your name?"

His laugh was a warm rumble against her ear. Castillo tightened his arm around her waist for a second, then patted her butt.

"Lieutenant Dominic Vincent Castillo, at your service."

Filled with something that if she wasn't too smart to know better, she'd call adoration, Lara smiled.

"Dominic, huh?" She let her mind adjust to that. For some reason, shifting from *Castillo* to *Dominic* was so intimate. Restless, she moved so her bare flesh slid over his naked skin, and acknowledged that maybe they'd crossed a line, that maybe now intimate was okay.

"Where do you live?" she asked, suddenly voracious for information about him. "Here? Is this your place or are we doing the bedtime boogie in someone else's bed?"

His laugh ruffled her hair.

"It's my bed but I don't know that I'd say I live here."

No wonder the place felt so impersonal. It was nice, luxurious even. But there were no pictures, no personal mementos sitting around for cursory snoops to find.

"Do you own the place?"

"Yeah."

"Does anyone else live in the house when you're not around?"

"Nope."

Lara had grown up surrounded by enough affluence not to question that someone would have a very nice house that they owned and left vacant for large periods of time.

"So where do you call home?"

"Wherever I'm assigned, I guess." He sounded as though he hadn't ever considered it before. "I mean, *home* home is where my family is. The ranch. But for me, I live on base most of the time."

"Which base are you stationed at?"

"Coronado. Southern California."

Which meant her brother was stationed there, too.

Lara tried to imagine Phillip as a California type.

Laid-back, surf savvy, noshing on nuts and berries.

It just didn't compute.

Maybe the whole military thing balanced out the chill California energy for him, kept it from being too fun.

Or maybe Phillip had changed.

Suddenly cold, Lara reached down to pull the blanket higher.

She hadn't let herself think about him. Not really.

Hadn't allowed worry to do more than creep around in the corners of her mind.

But here, in the dark, in the quiet, she had to ask.

"Is Phillip okay?"

"I don't know that I'd call him okay. He's kinda uptight and standoffish if you ask me."

Lara's smile was more a stiff shift of her lips than any attempt at humor.

"Seriously. Is he safe?" She swallowed a knot in her throat. "Alive?"

"Your brother is a trained SEAL." Dominic ran his hand down the back of her head, combing his fingers through her hair. "I wouldn't worry about it if I were you."

"I shouldn't worry about it because he's going to be fine? Or I shouldn't worry about it because he and I haven't talked in eight years and don't even have so much as a fake haul-it-out-for-holidays relationship?"

His hesitation was a tiny thing. If she hadn't been lying against his chest, she probably wouldn't even have realized he'd paused. But there was just a tiny second there when he held his breath before continuing. "Like I said, Banks is a well-trained member of the special forces. You don't have to worry about him."

"But you are." Lara shifted to cross her hands over his chest, staring at Dominic in the moonlight. "If you weren't worried, you wouldn't have come to get me."

"Not true. Protecting you is my assignment. A lot of our work is based on possibilities. We see a possibility we don't like, we eliminate it."

"And the possibility that got you assigned to protect my body?" she asked, her eyes on her finger as she swirled it through the fine hair dusting his chest.

Dominic reached down, angling his finger under her chin to tilt her face toward his.

"I can't tell you about the mission. It's an ongoing operation and until I'm told otherwise, it's classified. I can promise you, though, that your brother is one of the best I've seen. He knows what he's doing and he's got the finest team in existence covering his ass."

Lara wet her lips, not sure why she was so close to tears.

Phillip was a stranger to her. She had less connection to him than she had to the creep cadre that haunted the alley behind the casino each night.

But she couldn't stop the unreasonable fear tugging at her heart.

"He's really that good?"

"He's one of the best," Dominic assured her.

"I thought you didn't like him."

"I don't have to be buddies with a guy to want him covering my back."

And that, she supposed, was the highest of compliments.

"Besides, protecting your body is a pleasure. I should actually thank your brother."

"I'll bet your throat would choke on the words," Lara teased.

"What? You don't think I can be grateful?"

"No. I think you can be very grateful. But I know how guys think. You say thanks, you figure you're giving my brother that kind of power over you. Even an inadvertent favor is still a favor."

"Very true." Dominic's laugh was appreciative as his hands slid down her back to settle in the curve just above her butt. "So? You think he'd hold it over me?"

"Prince Perfect? Unless he's changed, he doesn't keep score. Nope, Phillip's too good for that."

For the first time in years, Lara realized that didn't bother her. Phillip being perfect was his cross to bear, not hers.

She sighed, hoping perfect got him through whatever he was dealing with. It couldn't be that bad, could it? He was a SEAL. He wouldn't settle for anything less. That had to mean something, right?

"Why'd you become a SEAL?" she asked, needing to talk about something else before she started thinking of Phillip as an actual, real brother or something crazy like that.

"Because nobody else in my family had."

"Right. I'll bet nobody else in your family is a circus clown, either, but I don't see you sporting polka dots and a red nose," Lara said, laughing.

"Actually, my uncle Manny is a rodeo clown. Close enough to keep me out of floppy shoes."

Giving him an impatient look, Lara tapped her fingers against his chest. Finally, he shrugged.

"Okay, really. I joined the Navy because nobody else had served in the military. In a family as big as mine, everyone has pretty much done everything by the time you get to it. When I hit college, I knew everything I didn't want to do but really had no clue what I did want."

"What happened?"

"I went home with a buddy on spring break. His brother was a Ranger."

"Ranger?"

"Army."

"But you joined the Navy."

"I like the water," he said with a laugh.

"That simple?" *Seriously? He's inspired by the brother of a friend and likes the water, and just like that, he's found his life calling?* Lara wasn't sure if she was impressed or jealous.

"I'm a simple guy. When something's right, I know it." He squeezed her butt. "Like this."

Good, delicious, mind-blowing, maybe.

But *right?*

Lara figured maybe he needed to check his thesaurus.

She and he? They were passing ships on that water he was so fond of.

She swallowed against the bitter taste coating her throat. That's just the way it was. Being upset about it was a waste of energy.

"What about you? You're all about the dance? Wasn't it just like that?" he asked, thankfully changing the subject.

"For a while," she acknowledged. To this day, Lara didn't know if it'd been passion that had driven her love of dance or a desperate need to immerse herself in something. Anything that made her feel good, accepted. And kept her away from her family as much as possible.

"You said something about Broadway, right?"

"Right. For two years."

"So is that what you always wanted to do? Dance?"

"Enough to leave home for it." Lara sighed, missing

that feeling. She'd had so much passion and belief in her dream. Nothing was going to stand in her way.

Except, of course, herself.

"That's why you left? You couldn't dance in Maryland?"

"Last time I looked, Broadway was in New York," she quipped. Then, seeing his impatient look, she relented. Fine, he wanted a peek into her past, she figured she owed him. "My parents were fine with me dancing, per se. It was a nice, ladylike hobby, acceptable among their society friends."

"I've gotta say, I'm having serious trouble picturing you as a meek, ladylike society girl."

"You and me both." Lara smiled, resting her chin on the hands she'd folded over his chest. "I loved the dance. Obsessed with it. It's all I wanted. But the rest? Country club socials, acceptable dates, polite well-rounded dinner conversation? I didn't quite live up to expectations. By the time I was sixteen, they figured my obsession with dance was getting in the way of my duties."

"They wanted you to stop?"

"They ordered me to quit. Refused to pay for classes, then grounded me six months later when they found out I was still going. I applied for a scholarship and you'd have thought I'd tried to murder my mother."

"Because you disobeyed?"

"Hardly. I rarely behaved to their standards anyway." Lara laughed. "No, she was furious because I'd implied that we needed financial assistance."

"And your brother?"

Lara frowned.

"What about him? He never weighed in on the discussion, if that's what you mean. I'm honestly not sure he realized I was a dancer. I'm positive he never noticed when I left."

"How is that possible? You lived in the same house, right?"

"Not really. I mean, technically we did. But he went to prep school, then Annapolis. My dance schedule got me out of boarding school, but it wasn't like I hung out at home watching TV and chatting with the parents."

"So you took off for Broadway? That's, like, fancy dancing, isn't it?"

"I suppose. Ballet, jazz, tap, I did it all." She smiled against his chest. "I was good."

"How good?" he asked.

She laughed at the innuendo, then shrugged.

"Really good, actually. I'd been dancing since I was a toddler, so I had a lot of time to work on it. By nineteen I was an up-and-comer. Another year, maybe two, I'd have been out of the corps and dancing solo roles."

"So how'd you get from there to Broadway to the Silver Dust?"

"Life took me on a trip," Lara said lightly.

She didn't want to talk about all her screwups, lousy choices or many failures. Not with a guy who probably had none of the above, and was probably going to turn out to be all of the above for her.

"Enough with tiptoeing through the past," she said, angling her body so she was over him instead of on his side. "Let's talk about something more interesting. Like nothing."

His hands skimmed from her hips upward, briefly cupping her breasts before sliding back down and between her thighs.

Oh, baby, he had talented fingers.

"Okay, but first I have to ask…"

Heart racing, desire curling in her belly and need clawing its way through her system, Lara shrugged.

"Fine. Ask fast, though."

Unfortunately, though, he apparently couldn't ask and play at the same time, because he moved his hand from her welcoming heat to her waist.

Dammit.

"You're up there on stage. Dancing. Almost naked. Thousands of strangers watch you each week."

Desire forgotten, Lara tensed. Was he seriously going to pull out the judgment card? Now? Her knee twitched as it calculated the distance to his groin.

"Isn't that hat heavy as hell?" he finally asked.

"What?"

"You're so graceful up there. You swerve, you sway, you kick and hop and dance all over. But you're wearing that big-ass hat. Isn't it heavy?"

Lara blinked.

That was it?

The relief pouring through her was almost as strong as the orgasm she'd relished earlier. Deep, penetrating and powerful enough to make her want to cry.

No judgment.

No pithy criticism of her parading near-naked for perverts, friends and strangers alike.

Nobody, ever in her life, had simply accepted her like that.

Lara didn't know what to think, what to do.

She almost kissed him. But that'd be admitting how much his opinion meant, and she wasn't stupid.

So she went for light and easy instead, figuring she'd show her gratitude in a silent, easily-misinterpreted-as-lust kind of way.

"Most of my headdresses weigh between eight and twelve pounds," she told him, tilting her head to one side, then the other as if balancing a hat.

"I'm impressed," he mused, his fingers skimming along the side of her head to chuck her under the chin. "Do they teach that in dance school?"

Lara laughed, thinking of the hours of grueling, sweat-inducing, body-twisting dance classes she'd attended over the years.

"Oddly enough, no. How to wear a heavy costume isn't covered in most dance curriculums. But thanks to my most excellent upper-body strength, I'm a natural." Showing off a little, and desperate to get his hands onto her body where they belonged, Lara flexed. "Wanna feel?"

"Impressive," he agreed, his fingers sliding over her bicep.

"And now that we've settled that, why don't we see if we can get you that hard," she challenged before reaching down to stroke his impressive muscle.

As they slid into a nice wave of lust, something Lara could easily understand and handle, she tucked away that feeling of acceptance. If a girl got used to that kind of thing, who knew what she might start wanting.

Scary things.

Like love.

9

LARA HAD SPENT most of her life on stage. She'd been stared at, had her movements dissected and her body critiqued. Her childhood had been a training ground for high-society head games. She'd dined with senators and in soup kitchens.

But nothing had prepared her for this.

She looked around the dining room with wide eyes. Someone had butted two long and narrow tables together to accommodate the masses of food. And the crowd.

It was a toss-up which of the two was more impressive.

Roast, potatoes, enchiladas, a delicious soup called posole and an array of vegetables to make any growing kid sprout up healthy. As colorful and tempting as all of that was, Lara had only managed a couple of bites because she was too distracted.

These people were loud.

Loud, and incredible-looking.

Life had clearly blessed the Castillo clan with a whole lot of gorgeous. The men were dark and big, a few towering over Dominic's impressive height. The women were stunning, from Nana Rosa to the baby beating her spoon on the other end of the table.

"So, Lara, right?" The exotic brunette with Castillo's eyes leaned around her brother to gesture with her fork. "Dom's never brought a girl home for Sunday dinner before. Where did you two meet?"

Thankfully, Lara had finally lifted the forkful of food to her mouth, so she had the excuse of chewing to gather her thoughts.

Dominic had told her to feel comfortable, be at home and enjoy his family. He'd also reminded her that she was his mission, and that meant top secret.

Fine by her.

"Dominic saw me dance," she said instead. Then she slanted the man next to her a teasing look and added, "As soon as he did, he was smitten. He practically begged me to get coffee with him."

"And did you get coffee with him?" Celia asked, her eyes narrowed. Lara didn't understand why she seemed so suspicious.

"Lara played hard to get," Dominic interjected, laying his arm over the back of Lara's chair and giving her an indulgent look. "But I convinced her. Eventually."

"Eventually," Celia repeated, her tone delighted. "Good for you, Lara. That's the first time I've ever heard him having to beg for anything. Girls have always made things too easy for this one. It's about time he had to work a little."

"Hey, you're supposed to be on my side," Dominic protested.

"Yeah, Celia. You're supposed to regale Lara with stories about how great Dominic is," a man said from across the table. "Isn't that right, little brother?"

"I'd rather hear Lara's stories." Celia's smile was all friendly curiosity. "So you dance? Where?"

Lara glanced at her plate, debating for a brief second. She liked Dominic's family. They had all offered a friendly welcome and, despite their obvious curiosity, had made her feel comfortable and appreciated.

Dominic was clearly the golden boy, the pride of the family. How would they feel knowing the woman he'd brought home was one step up from a stripper?

She waited for Dominic to interrupt, to tell his version of their meeting. Because she wouldn't lie.

But he didn't say anything.

Okay, fine. Deep breath, big smile and showtime.

"I'm a showgirl," Lara said, meeting Celia's eyes with a direct look. "I dance at the Silver Dust Casino in Reno."

"Really? Do you train for that kind of dancing?" Celia asked, not even blinking.

Lara frowned.

Where was the judgment?

"Um, not really. I mean, I had extensive training before I got to Reno, but I never trained as a showgirl."

"What kind of dance did you do before?"

"She was on Broadway," Dominic broke in. Lara blinked at the pride in his voice. As if he thought it was a really big deal. From the impressed looks around the table, a lot of the rest of his family thought so, too.

"Hey, we just saw a dancer the other night," said one of Dominic's cousins sitting halfway down the table. "Marco's bachelor party. Her name was Lotta Oomph, and boy, did she live up to it. She had the hots for Dom, too."

Lara's lips twitched, and she slanted Dominic a glance.

He shrugged and gave her a look as if to say, *what's a guy to do?*

"Enough, Leon." Dominic's mother shot her nephew a chiding look, then lifted a platter. "Lara, would you like more empanadas?"

"Thank you." Lara took the platter. "Everything is delicious."

"Don't you have to watch your weight as a dancer?" Celia asked, giving Lara's plate an envious look. "I only did ballet for a year, but I thought I was going to starve."

"I don't usually eat much," Lara acknowledged. Not because of her weight, but because she couldn't afford a lot of food. "But I have a pretty fast metabolism."

"So does Dom." Celia sniffed at her brother. "I could almost hate him for that if he wasn't so great."

"That must be pretty cool, having a brother you think is great."

"I have four of them," Celia said, her tone making it clear she wasn't picking favorites. "Lucas is the best at fixing things and Matteo is the funniest. Dominic knows everything, though. You want advice, you talk to him. He always has the answers."

Lara noticed she didn't mention a fourth name. A quick glance around the table and she realized that whoever their other brother was, he wasn't here tonight.

Of course, who was she to comment on familial relationships or question fallings-out?

"Dominic said you wanted the security code for internet access," Lucas said, taking the platter and sliding four empanadas onto his plate. "I can give it to you after dinner."

"Thanks. I have homework due Monday and want to make sure it's in." Lara tasted the empanada. *Oh, my.* The meat-filled pastry was so delicious that her mouth exploded in delight.

"What're you in school for?" Lucas asked.

"You're in school?" Dominic muttered at the same time.

Lara slid him a sideways look, but responded to Lucas instead. "I'm studying computer security with Fireside Tech," she told him. "This is my last semester."

"Fireside?" For the first time since they'd gathered at

the table, Lucas put his fork down. "They're good. Are you specializing?"

"I've got top marks in home security and systems design, but I'd really like to get into cybersecurity. That's what I'm focused on the most." Lara's voice trailed off when she realized everyone had quieted and was now staring at her and Lucas. Suddenly as self-conscious as she'd be if she were wearing her feather costume and dancing on the table, Lara gave a little shrug and finished with, "That's about it."

"Really?"

Before she could tell Dominic, "Yes, *really,*" Lucas broke in.

"What do you know about the Onyx R300 system?"

What did *he* know about it?

Too confused to be rude, Lara explained how she'd reprogrammed the Onyx home security system the previous semester in the school lab in order to overwrite a common weather glitch.

"You fixed that? The company said it couldn't be done. That's why they had issues with the Onyx R500 this summer." Lucas gave her a long look, then nodded to her plate. "You finished?"

Lara glanced down. She'd barely eaten half her dinner, but now she was too intrigued to want more, so she nodded.

"Mama, excuse us," Lucas said, getting up from the table and gesturing for Lara to join him.

"Dessert?" Mrs. Castillo asked, not looking at all surprised that one of her sons was leaving dinner with another son's girlfriend. No, not girlfriend. Date. Guest? Lara pressed her lips together, too confused to figure out what she and Dominic were now.

"What's dessert?" Lucas asked, pausing on his way out the door.

"Chocolate cake, cherry pie or flan."

"Save us some—" He arched a glance at Lara.

"Cake, please."

"Save us some cake."

He gestured for her to follow. After a baffled glance back at Dominic, who just sat and grinned, Lara did.

Three hours later, she slid onto the bench seat of the truck Dominic had traded his bike for. He waited for her to settle in, then closed the door before going around to the driver's side to get in himself.

"Your family is pretty awesome," she told him as he started the engine.

"They think you're pretty awesome, too."

They do?

The words were almost out of her mouth before she realized it. Instead of asking such a needy question, Lara rested her head on the seat back and watched the lights of the house and outbuildings fade into the distance.

His family actually liked her.

What an odd concept.

Her own family didn't think she was awesome.

Maybe that's why she had never once, in her seventeen years with them, relaxed and simply enjoyed herself the way she had tonight.

She'd talked security systems with Lucas.

Discussed dance with Celia.

Mrs. Castillo had given her the posole recipe, insisting that a pot of soup could keep a pretty girl like her in meals for a week. Lara still wasn't sure what hominy was, but she was going to give it a try.

Wow.

What a weekend.

Incredible sex, followed by the attack of the goon guy. A motorcycle ride through scenic California, then more incredible sex. An entire day of even more incredible sex. Then that dinner.

Enjoying the smooth satisfaction, Lara followed Dominic out of the truck and into his cabin. Inside, he hit that button that locked the place up again. It made sense now—his home was protected by the best Castillo Security had to offer. She barely resisted asking if she could poke around his security panel.

"You look happy," he said, tossing his keys on the counter. "You have fun tonight?" Hands empty now, he reached out and pulled her close.

"Yeah," she said. "I did have fun."

Lara's smile shifted from satisfied to seductive as she leaned into Dominic's body. His chest was hard against her breasts, his thighs braced as if he was ready to rock.

"How fun?" he asked in a husky tone, his hands cupping her butt to pull her tight against his growing erection. Lara gave a little hip swivel, just to up the stakes, then brushed her lips over his.

"Fun enough that I don't know how you're going to top it tonight," she said against his mouth.

Dominic swiped his tongue over her lips, then said, "Why don't we see what I can come up with?"

LARA HAD A way with fun.

Sexy fun.

Sweet fun.

Chocolate-covered fun.

And, dammit, the kind of fun that sneaked under a guy's skin. Which was why he hadn't been able to resist staying here for the week instead of taking her down to Coronado.

From outside, Dominic watched her and his sister through the window of his cabin. Their laughter rang out the open door; their smiles lit in the dim morning light.

"They're having fun."

He glanced at Lucas, who had his head under the hood of the truck. Paranoid as ever, he figured it needed a once-over before it could handle the trip south.

"She's had fun with everyone this week," he observed in return.

"Ma likes her." Lucas's words echoed through the engine compartment, taking on an otherworldly blessing tone.

Ma liked her. Grandma liked her. Matteo, Lucas—everyone liked her.

But she and Celia had gotten tightest.

God knew what they whispered about. It wasn't all clothes, although his sister had taken a trip into Sacramento to get Lara what she deemed a dozen bags full of essentials. Lara had been upset that he'd covered the cost, but had settled when he told her he'd add it to Banks's tab.

Then she'd laughed.

She laughed a lot more now than she had when they'd first met. Over the past few days, she'd actually started to glow. It wasn't the attention that was making her look more relaxed and happy than he'd seen her in their weeklong relationship. For all her lack of inhibitions and ease onstage, attention actually seemed to make her uncomfortable.

She liked his family.

Not a surprise, since Dominic considered his family pretty damned awesome. Meantime her only living relative was one certified stick-in-the-mud, Lieutenant Phillip Banks.

Poor girl.

As if he had a wiretap hooked up to Dominic's brain, Lucas looked out from under the hood and asked, "So you know her brother, right?"

Not really.

He could pick him out of a lineup, write a job recommendation for the guy. But know him?

"We serve together," was all he could say, hoping Lucas would get the hint and change the subject.

"You gonna bring her back?"

Not even close to the change Dominic had been hoping for.

"I dunno. I'm not really in a relationship place."

"Who is?"

"Women?"

"Not that one," Lucas said with a laugh, tilting his head toward the cabin.

"No?" Dominic frowned at the cabin.

Lara didn't want a relationship?

At all? Or with him?

How did Lucas know that?

Dominic almost asked, then decided he really didn't want to know.

He tossed his duffel behind the truck seat. He didn't have much to pack. Pretty much everything he needed was on base. But it didn't hurt to bring a few dozen extra condoms, a bottle of hot fudge and his digital camera, too. Not that he wanted to make dirty movies with Lara. Much. But he figured a few pictures of her visit to San Diego and Coronado would be fun to have.

A little souvenir of their time together.

He stared blankly at the trees on the other side of the truck, wondering why. He'd never wanted anything to remember a relationship by before. And if Lucas was right, Lara had no interest in one, either.

So why was he so reluctant to let go of this one? It'd been a week. Usually at this point he was done, finished and ready to be long gone. If he even made it this far. Most women had issues with the idea of his job being top secret, or that he'd be gone indefinitely. They figured a guy was cheating or didn't care enough. He'd always considered it one of his greatest job benefits.

Now he was wondering how the guys in relationships made it work. Masters and Lane were both recently married and seemed to juggle it all just fine. Then again, their ladies were rare and special. Same with Landon. He'd been married over a year—a record for some military guys.

"You're good to go," Lucas decided, slamming the hood shut and giving it a pat. He tilted his head toward the house. "I'm gonna get Celia and go. You good?"

"I'm good." Dominic issued his traditional response, slapped his brother on the back, then lifted the cooler his mom had filled into the truck.

While Lucas went inside to say his goodbyes and drag their sister away, Dominic reminded himself that he wasn't looking for a relationship.

He just wanted to help Lara out.

He had a few ideas. First he'd have to find her a better job to keep her going until she was through with school. Something she could do with a few extra clothes on. And there was no point finding her a new apartment until she knew where she wanted to work. Maybe she'd get crazy for Southern California and want to relocate there. If her apartment was close to base, he could visit from time to time.

Damn.

Dominic all but smacked himself in the head.

There he went again, thinking those ridiculous relationship thoughts.

Not gonna happen.

He was gonna fix things up for Lara, then this was over.

Bad Ass had messaged the night before with news.

Bird in hand, flying back to nest.

The team should be in Coronado within a day, debriefed and available within the week.

Dominic could have simply returned Lara to Reno with the news about her brother. Fixed her apartment door, kissed her cheek and let her get back to her life.

That's what he should have done.

Instead, he'd told her they'd be safer on base.

True, but now totally inapplicable to the situation.

But he figured she'd already called work to arrange to take the rest of the week off, so they might as well go. They'd cruise down the coast, spend more time together, have enough sex that he'd get her out of his system.

He was due back on duty the first of next week, so by the time they'd come up for air he'd be ready to put her on a plane back to Reno.

If she ever got out here. Dominic looked at his watch, then the cabin door.

As if she heard his impatience, Lara sauntered out, duffel over her shoulder and a laugh on her lips. His brother and sister flanked her, but he barely saw them.

Damn.

She was crazy sexy.

Long, leggy and slender, her body was a work of art that he was afraid he could spend forever studying. She'd fancied up her simple jeans and a long-sleeved tee as green as her eyes by adding a scarf that draped around and around her neck in a fluffy circle. The filmy blue fabric somehow highlighted instead of hid her full breasts. Dominic liked that in fashion.

He waited for the goodbyes, barely offering more than a cursory hug and nod to his family to hurry them along.

"Sorry, I was just thanking Celia and Lucas," she said, her ever-present laptop tight in her hand. "You have the nicest family. Did you know she came over to hang out last night while you and Lucas were off doing your boy-club powwow?"

"Yeah, she said she was going to." Ready to hit the road, he opened the passenger door, waiting until she was settled before circling the truck. As he started the engine, he glanced over, taking another second to appreciate his sister's choice in clothes if she'd had a hand in what Lara was wearing. "She likes you."

"She's great." Lara spent the next twenty minutes chatting about his family. Impressions, observations, questions.

It was cute.

"Lucas figures you're gonna nail the security tech internship." Waiting for the light to signal that they were clear to turn onto the freeway, Dominic reached over to flick Lara's scarf, just there by the tip of her breast. "He's trying to figure out how to change your mind and get you to come on board with Castillo Security instead."

He grinned when he saw that her nipple had hardened against her T-shirt. Damn, she was delicious.

Lara twisted around, one knee on the seat between them as she reached over to grab his arm. She didn't seem interested in her body's reaction, though.

"He really said that?" Lara's laugh sounded more stunned than amused as she reached over to lay her hand on his arm.

He looked at her fingers with a frown, realizing this was the first sign of vulnerability he'd seen in her. After everything she'd been through, this got to her?

Dominic prided himself on knowing women. What made them tick, what got them happy, what turned them to mush.

But Lara kept on surprising him.

"Yeah." He shot her a glance. "Why the disbelief?"

Didn't you say you're top of your class? That means you're good, right?"

"Well, sure," she said with a shrug. "But good and good enough for a company like Castillo Security are two different things. Why didn't you tell me before that your family owned the biggest security company on the West Coast?"

"Sorry. I rarely think to share that with women." Or his assignments.

"Well, you should. It's pretty impressive."

Dominic gave her a baffled look.

"Lara, I'm a Navy SEAL. You really think I need to work to impress women?"

Lara's laughter burst out, filling the cab of the truck and making him grin.

She was tough, savvy, strong.

She was sexy, gorgeous and demanding.

And she had one hell of a sense of humor.

No.

Dominic stopped that thought in its tracks.

That was crazy thinking. It was just the novelty of seeing a woman around his family.

The ultimate challenge of fixing her life so it was as great as she deserved.

It was sex.

Just sex.

Dominic settled into the seat, one hand on the wheel and the other arm stretched across the bench seat so he could play with the short ends of Lara's hair. As the miles passed, he plotted.

She needed family.

He knew where she had one.

Time to fix that little rift, whatever it was, and give her that connection she craved.

Then he could get over this crazy idea of sharing his.

Because thinking like that, it was purely stupid.

That was the kind of thinking that led to expectations, sharing closet space and, God forbid, long-term commitment.

Nope.

Tension faded, leaving Dominic to focus on his fallback emotion toward women: affectionate lust. Yeah. That's all he felt for Lara.

And as long as he ignored that laughing voice in the back of his head, everything would be just fine.

"So tell me about your family."

Lara's gaze ricocheted off the soothing view of fields and trees to stare at Dominic. Frowning, she gave him an irritated look he didn't see because, of course, he was driving.

"Why?" Talking about them would ruin the nice mood she'd been in.

"Because I'm curious. C'mon, you know everything about mine. Don't tell me my grandmother didn't show you that picture frame with all of my school photos. Kindergarten to graduation, with a story for every year."

Lara's annoyance faded a little as she recalled his second-grade picture. He'd been so cute with his front teeth missing and his hair in little-punk-boy spikes.

"I liked your prom pictures better," she said, shifting in her seat and reaching over to tap his thigh with her fingers. "So did you get lucky with that cute little blonde?"

"Which one? I went to three proms."

"All with blondes?"

"What can I say, it was a phase," he said with a shrug. Then he shot her a laughing look. "I'm partial to brunettes now, though."

"You're partial to anything female, you mean. Don't try to deny it. I talked to at least twenty members of your family this week and every one had a story about you and a girl. But no two were the same girl."

"So I know how you went from Maryland to New York, but how did you end up in Reno?" he asked, surprising her.

"You want to know how I ended up a showgirl, you mean?"

"Sure, maybe. I'm not criticizing, I'm just curious. Broadway indicates some major dedication. So why would you leave it?"

"I had to." Lara shifted in her seat, wishing he'd talk about something else. She hated thinking about what she'd given up. It wasn't that she was so dedicated that she mourned leaving something she'd spent most of her life training for. No, she just hated the reminder of why she'd lost it all.

Especially now, when she was head over heels for a guy who'd end up leaving her high and dry.

But this time she wasn't sidelining her dreams or giving up her ambitions. She'd used the extra time off work to finish her homework and her semester project and to grill Lucas for information that should help her ace her final exam. For once a relationship was actually working in her favor.

"So what happened to make you leave Broadway?" he asked again, interrupting her self-congratulatory mental happy dance.

"Life. She has a way of stepping in and shaking things up, you know. I figure it's her way of keeping us from getting too cocky." She angled an arch look his way. "You should watch out. I'll bet you're due."

"C'mon, tell me. You know everything about me," he

reminded her. "Including the sad fact that I wore a purple tuxedo to the prom."

"It was closer to violet," she observed. Then she shrugged. "It's not a very exciting story. I was in a car accident. Busted my leg up pretty bad."

He shot her a frown. "You didn't call your parents? Go home, play good daughter for a while until you healed?"

"I called them," she said stiffly.

"And?"

"They said I'd made my choice, now I could live with it." Lara's words were matter-of-fact. She'd expected nothing less, nothing more. After all, she'd left home for a reason. Why would her being gone change anything?

"Son of a bitch," Dominic breathed. His fingers clenched, stretched then clenched again on the steering wheel. "Banks left you swinging in the wind, too?"

"Phillip?" Lara blinked. Had she ever considered calling him back then? She tried to remember, but didn't recall that ever entering her head.

"You didn't even ask him for help?"

"I never thought about it. He was always a toe-the-line kind of guy, though. No reason to think Prince Perfect would buck the company line."

"That's just sibling rivalry," Dominic said with an indulgent glace that made Lara want to punch him. "Everyone who has brothers or sisters has that. Doesn't mean he wouldn't have helped you."

She rolled her eyes. As if he had a clue?

"Enough talking about ancient history," she dismissed with a wave of her hand. "Tell me what we're going to do when we get to Southern California."

He shot her a look that said he was doing her a favor but would be returning to the subject later. Fine. Lara knew how to dodge with the best of them.

"When we get to Southern California?" he mused. "We're going to have sex. Lots and lots of crazy, wild sex."

Sounded good to her.

10

WHAT A MONTH.

Two weeks ago, she hadn't known Dominic Castillo existed.

Now she was sitting on a hotel terrace overlooking the Pacific Ocean, sipping coffee and debating her newfound attitude and how she felt about it.

Southern California's much too laid-back attitude seemed to be rubbing off on her. Two days after arriving, he'd gone back on duty, but they still spent every night together, had gone sightseeing and spent glorious hours on the beach. Who knew she was crazy about the ocean? With Dominic on duty during the day, she had plenty of time to add extras to her final project. Nights were for wild sex, long walks on the beach and soulful talks. She figured the wild sex balanced out the cheesiness of the other two.

When Flo had called to reluctantly inform her that she'd been fired, Lara had just laughed.

Nibbling a strawberry, the sweetly tart juice exploding on her tongue, Lara watched the tiny surfers from afar.

Her landlord had left a message with Flo that she was evicted. Apparently he hadn't found a body in her apartment so didn't feel her excuse was justified and was keeping her deposit but throwing away her belongings. No biggie, since Lara didn't figure they could scrape together enough of that mess to equal a single thing worth saving.

So she was jobless and homeless.

And she was oddly fine with that. It was as though a huge weight of obligation was gone. Of course, she had very little money and no apparent means of making more until she graduated. Since the internship paid jack, she'd have to find some way to cover the bills. But she couldn't quite work up enough energy to worry.

Lara's easy mood dimmed.

She was a little worried for her brother. Dominic had assured her over and over that Phillip was fine, that she just had to lay low a little longer while the team secured the situation. But now, after barely thinking about the guy more than a dozen times over the years, she was thinking of him daily. She could chalk that up to the situation. After all, it was because of him that she was here on this very balcony.

But that didn't explain why she was suddenly wondering how he was doing. What he was like. Did he still eat his cereal dry and read at the table when he was alone? Did he ever think about the Christmas their parents had spent in Vail, leaving the two of them home alone? They'd had McDonald's for breakfast because neither could cook and Phillip had driven Lara to the store the next day to exchange all of her lousy gifts. She'd totally forgotten about those things until this month.

She'd almost forgotten what he looked like, his image flashes of photographs rather than impressions of his actual self.

Now she wondered.

Late at night, curled in Dominic's arms, she pondered if she'd ever find out. If she'd have a chance to.

And why it was suddenly so important.

Lara poured more coffee, drinking it fast to wash away the worry. Using the same guaranteed method of calming herself that she'd employed all week, Lara took a deep breath, cleared her mind, then imagined Dominic naked.

Oh, yeah...

Hard muscles. Golden skin. Big blue eyes and those sexy man dimples. Long, erect delight.

Worked like a charm.

Soothed and happy again, Lara settled her feet on the balcony railing, wondering if—brotherly worries aside— she'd ever been this happy.

Especially considering that she was pretty much positive that she'd done the stupidest thing of her life. She'd fallen in love with Dominic Castillo. And the weird thing was, that didn't bother her, either.

She should be terrified.

She should be freaking out.

This was scarier than those goons breaking into her apartment, the one who'd grabbed her and the creep cadre all balled together.

If she were smart, she'd be hitchhiking back to Reno or New York or, hell, even Maryland.

She shouldn't be chilling on the balcony of a hotel room that she couldn't afford to pay for, eating fattening croissants and thinking about complex HTML code and various sexual positions.

Lara broke off a piece of pastry, the buttery flakes melting on her tongue as she contemplated it all.

Yeah.

She'd probably slipped around the edge into crazyville.

She didn't take things easy.

She didn't do calm and reasonable.

Hell, she didn't even relax.

Something to blame Castillo for, she decided.

Through the open patio door she heard the swoosh of the hotel room door closing and sighed, pleasure curling around peace in her stomach.

She didn't need to look to know it was Dominic. It was as if she could sense him now. A little voice in Lara's head screamed *WTF,* and she imagined that tiny screamer beating on the walls of her brain, trying to wake the real her up. But she was so happy, that voice was easy to ignore.

A hand, warm and hard, slid over her bare shoulder.

"Hi." She tilted her head to rub her cheek over his hand, then grinned when it slid past her shoulder onto her breast. "Aw, now, Jimmy, I told you I only tip like that for chocolate. Coffee and croissants don't merit copping a feel."

"Cute." Grinning, Dominic came around to drop into the chair next to her. He snagged a pastry from the basket and popped it into his mouth. While he chewed, Lara let her gaze wander over his excellent form. Clad in fatigues and a tee, paratrooper-style black boots and a camo cap, he must be on a break, not off duty.

Even while she appreciated the view, her lips moved into a half pout. A break meant no sexy times, but seeing him in his military clothes was enough of a turn-on to keep her revved until bedtime. Or at least until six, when he'd walk through the door again for dinner.

"You like it here?" he asked.

Surprised, Lara tilted her sunglasses down to get a better look at his face. Nary a dimple was showing, so he must be serious.

"Here? On the balcony? Here at the hotel? Here in California?" She arched one brow. "Wanna narrow it down?"

"Here. Southern California, close to the base."

Lara wet her lips, excitement bubbling a nervous brew in her belly.

"Why?"

"I asked first."

"Yeah, but if you don't answer first, you won't find out, will you?" She shot him an arch smile.

"You always get the upper hand that way?" he asked, pouring a cup of coffee and toasting her.

"By being clever? Yeah, it usually works." She waited, but he didn't tell her what he was talking about. Clearly, he thought he could out-stubborn clever.

Lara waited until he reached for another pastry, then took the basket just before he could get one.

"You were saying why you wanted to know if I like it here?" she encouraged with a smile.

He gave her a hard stare, looked at the basket, then at her again.

"Curious," he finally said.

Lara shifted the basket so it was on the edge of the balcony, one quick tip from taking a twenty-story header.

"Just wondering if you might want to stick around," he said, his expression somewhere between irritated and impressed. "Maybe meet a few people, hang out a little. You're done with your final project, right? So you have some time?"

See. Clever. She knew her man, knew his weaknesses. Dominic didn't have many, but unless it was a military secret, he was all about the food.

Lara handed him the pastry basket, then shrugged.

"I'm technically done with the project, but I'd like to add a few more things. I'd love to ask Lucas some advice, though. Can I get his number?"

Yet another odd change.

Lara was used to working alone.

She thrived on her own energy and figured if she ever

got a tattoo, it'd read something like Me, Myself and I—why mess with perfection?

But it'd been so cool to talk shop with Lucas.

And *shopping* with Celia.

But she hadn't thought to get their phone numbers when she was there, and she hadn't managed to get them from Dominic yet.

His frown came and went so fast she could almost convince herself she'd imagined it. Almost. Why didn't he want her talking to his brother?

"I'll get it for you later. First, though, how about some fun?"

Lara gave a sexy hum, sliding her hand up his thigh. Before she got to anything interesting, he grinned.

"That's fun, but not quite what I meant. How does dinner out sound?" His fingers teased the edge of her hair in a gesture more sweet than sexual that turned her on all the same. "A few buddies, their wives, margaritas and nachos."

Lara's mellow went poof.

Tension ratcheted down her spine and her teeth clenched.

She was having a great time with Dominic, and yes, falling for him was more fact than fiction now.

But getting sucked into his life? Hanging out with his friends? Especially military types who probably knew her brother? That freaked her out more than meeting his family had.

She didn't know why, but it did.

What were the chances of his friends actually liking her? She wasn't riding the pity train, but she wasn't exactly the cute-and-cuddly type. Hell, even her parents hadn't liked her.

And she knew how these things worked. Dominic would say he didn't care, that they didn't have to hang with his friends. But she'd heard him talk about his team—she knew how close these guys were. When push came to shove, he'd pick his friends.

Her stomach knotted as disappointment wrapped its way through her.

If this was his surprise, it kinda sucked.

Anger breaking through her mellow, she dropped her feet to the ground so fast the collar of her robe slid down, baring her shoulder.

Before she could snap at him, Dominic's smile shifted, his eyes going hot.

Lara wet her lips.

He set down his coffee.

Perfect.

Was distracting her man with sex something she was proud of? Lara debated for all of two seconds before she decided that, hell, yeah, hot sex was a win-win.

So distract away.

She leaned forward to grab a jar off the table, making sure to hunch her shoulders so her robe gaped enough to play peekaboo.

"I think I finally figured out why they sent jam with the pastries," she said in a slow, musing tone. His eyes tracked her moves as she dipped her finger into the ornate jar, then lifted it to her mouth.

And sucked.

A little smile played around his mouth so his dimples danced, and Lara melted a little.

Damn, those dimples were lethal.

Lara dipped her finger again, scooping up more of the sticky red sweetness.

She made as if to give Dominic a taste, but at the last second, just when she saw his tongue, she pulled her hand back and laughed.

Even as she teased, desire grabbed hold of her. It was an addiction, so heady and strong she didn't think she'd ever get enough.

"Hey," he protested.

"My breakfast, my treat."

"You're not big on sharing?"

"Depends on what's in it for me," she said honestly.

"Pleasure like you've never experienced before?" he offered softly.

"Oh, but I've experienced a whole lot of pleasure. You'd have to work awfully hard at topping what we've done already," she told him, getting even more turned on thinking about some of their adventures.

Dominic reached for her, but Lara was quick and danced out of reach.

"Bet I can," he promised.

"Bet I can first," she challenged.

To prove she could, she held her jam-covered finger up at the same time she used the other hand to unknot the belt of her robe.

Lara lifted one shoulder so the silk slid down, exposing a bare breast. She paused long enough to give him a good look, then switched so the silk slid the other way. It caught for a second on her pebbled nipple, making Dominic groan softly.

Lara stepped forward until she was standing right between his legs. Eyes hot, he reached up. She stepped back and shook her head.

"No touching," she murmured.

Tormenting was more fun that way.

"You're playing with fire," he warned, his hotly gleaming eyes echoing that statement.

"Well, then, let's see how hot I can get it."

It only took a twitch of her shoulders to send her robe

plummeting. The fabric caught on her elbows, framing her nude body. Lara's gaze locked on his, so when she glanced down his eyes automatically followed.

Lara slid her jelly-covered finger over her nipple, noting with artistic appreciation that the sticky treat matched perfectly. She took her time, rubbing it around and around to ensure she was sugared up.

With every swirl of her fingers, desire coiled tighter in her belly. Her nipple was hard beneath her finger, her breath short.

Dominic's hands didn't leave his thighs, but when his fingers clenched as if he were forcing himself to stay still, she lifted her finger to her mouth.

"Mmm," she moaned as she licked—not sucked—the rest of the jelly clean. Her tongue swirled up her finger, her eyes locked on Dominic.

"Want some?" she whispered as she stepped closer.

Close enough that all he'd have to do was stick out his tongue to get a taste.

"I want," he confirmed in a guttural tone. "You know we're in public, though, right?"

Lara didn't bother looking around. It'd take someone with wings or high-powered binoculars to see anything worth getting excited about.

"Shy?" she teased.

"I was thinking of you."

"Oh, because I'm such a modest girl?"

Laughing at the idea, Lara let the robe fall the rest of the way to the patio, standing naked in front of him except for her jelly coating.

"C'mon, big boy," she taunted. "Show me what you've got."

His eyes not leaving hers, Dominic reached down. She heard a snap, a zipper, then fabric sliding down. Lara wet her lips, wanting to look but not willing to be the first to shift her gaze.

Out of the corner of her eye, she saw his hands moving, knew he was pulling on a condom. She still didn't look down, though, liking the extra edge their staring contest added.

As soon as he stilled, she moved.

Straddling him, she locked her ankles behind his back, her heels digging into the seat of the chair for leverage.

Slowly, using muscles honed strong from years of daily dance, Lara lowered, impaling herself on his rock-hard cock. She slid down a millimeter at a time, her core muscles tight, her wet juices coating the way.

Her eyes still on his, Lara gripped Dominic's shoulders for balance. When he moved, just a small thrust, she shook her head.

"Mine," she instructed.

God, she loved challenging him. Loved even more that he let her take control.

His jaw tight, he looked as though he was struggling not to grab her and flip their positions. But after a second, he gave a jerky nod.

Lara grinned.

Big bad sexy SEAL was teetering on the edge of control.

She liked that.

It was incredible to realize that she'd pushed him there.

Then he got sneaky.

His eyes didn't leave hers as he leaned down a little to take her nipple into his mouth.

Lara whimpered.

Desire exploded, shooting in and out, spinning through her from her core to her nipples. Her heart raced; her thighs shook.

He tweaked the other with his fingers, then reached between them to work her the way only he could.

Lara bit her lip, trying to keep her rhythm steady.

But need was getting tighter, coiling like a spring deep in her belly.

Dominic lifted his head and grinned.

Dammit, he knew he was winning.

Lara leaned forward and licked his bottom lip, then sucked it between her teeth.

His eyes glazed.

She changed her rhythm, sliding, undulating, swirling and using her hips as though he was a stripper pole.

His breath came faster.

Lara was right there on the edge. She could barely focus because passion was demanding its due.

The only thing that kept the orgasm at bay was sheer stubborn will.

She wanted—no, she needed—to know that she could do to Dominic what nobody else could. She was desperate to know that she could do him in a way that would cement her in his memory, forever making him remember her as the girl who broke his control.

Pulling her hands off his shoulders, she arched her back, cupping her breasts in each hand and lifting them as an offering.

"Damn," he breathed. Just before he exploded.

With a keening cry, Lara flew after him. Her orgasm racked her body with tremors so strong she could barely keep her balance.

She didn't know how long it took, how many times she came.

All she knew was that when she opened her eyes, Dominic was grinning, his hands covering hers and his face totally relaxed.

Yeah. She was in love.

But she felt too good to care.

DOMINIC LAY ON his back, breathing as though he'd just hiked ten miles through the desert with a twenty-pound pack on his back—on water rations.

Damn.

First the balcony, now the bed. Two hot sessions in less than an hour. Hell of a morning break.

Every time he thought things between them couldn't get any hotter, Lara took it up a notch. A few more of her notches and she just might kill him.

But what a way to go.

He couldn't remember ever being this fascinated, this hooked, on a woman before.

Hell, he couldn't remember spending three weeks with the same woman before, either. What was it about Lara?

He sure wished he could figure it out.

The sooner he did, the sooner he could get his fill and move on.

The trouble was, it didn't seem to be any one thing.

At this rate, it might take forever to get his fill.

He reached over, his hand rubbing the soft flesh of her back where it dipped.

Then, with a deep breath, he smacked her butt before angling to a sitting position.

"Damn, you make break time great," he said. "I'm gonna grab a shower, then head back to base. I'll pick you up around seven for dinner, okay?"

Lara opened her mouth as if she wanted to protest, then she snapped it shut again.

"What?"

She frowned before sliding from the bed to grab her robe off the floor. Dominic watched her long limbs as she bent over, deciding that no matter what angle, she simply didn't have a bad view.

"Is Phillip back yet? Safe?" she asked as she belted the flimsy silk.

Dominic debated. She'd asked that same question daily since they'd arrived in Coronado. It wasn't as if it was classified information, so he had no reason for not telling her.

Except that the minute he did, he knew his hold on her was gone. She had no reason to think he was protecting her if her brother was safe.

Despite the fact that it flew in the face of his plan to give her that family connection, he'd been able to justify it for the first week while the team returned, then over the few days of debriefing. But now? Keeping it from her simply made him a creep. A desperate creep, at that.

Dominic sighed, running his hand over the short stubble of his freshly buzzed hair.

All of a sudden, he felt very naked.

Reminding himself that he was his most convincing in the nude, he offered Lara a charming smile.

"He's safe. Back on base, even."

He waited for her to ask to see Banks.

He half expected her to grab her duffel, shove her clothes in, tuck that laptop under her arm and wave goodbye.

But all she did was stare.

Green eyes didn't blink as she slowly frowned.

Dominic had an urge to grab a blanket off the bed.

"Lara?"

She wet her lips, then tilted her head as if to say, "What?"

"You heard me, right? He's back. He's fine."

Fine being relative, of course.

Banks had withstood some pretty intense questioning.

The kind that came with a side of torture. The guy had never been what anyone would call chatty, but the past few days in the barracks he'd taken silence to new levels.

He was hurting, even though he denied it.

He was suffering, even though it didn't show.

The guy couldn't have made it through debriefing without a psych eval, so he was either as fine as he said or a hell of an actor.

Dominic called it bullshit.

Which meant Banks needed help.

He needed family.

Just like his sister did.

"He's not going to this little dinner party you have planned, is he?" Lara asked, crossing her arms over her chest and shooting her hip to the side in a straight-up combative post. Dominic had been in combat enough to recognize the vibe, even if it was wrapped in blue silk.

He damn near sighed.

He was a man who appreciated the simple, the easy.

He had a reputation for bouncing from hot chick to wild woman to sexy siren, all without a hint of conflict.

And here he was, smack-dab in the middle of it.

Naked.

For the life of him, he couldn't figure out why.

All he knew was he wouldn't—couldn't—walk away from Lara.

Not yet.

"I wouldn't say your brother and I are on margarita terms," he finally said with a shrug. "I figured Bad Ass, Genius and maybe Boy Scout if he's around. I'd be happy to invite your brother if you want."

Seeing the look on her face, knowing exactly what was going through her mind, Dominic added, "Or if you're not up for a group thing, we can do dinner. Just you, me and Banks."

As threats went, it was pretty good.

Lara wrinkled her nose and gave a delicate shudder before shaking her head. "I told you before, I don't want to see Phillip. So margaritas are fine," she stated. She made a show of glancing at the bedside clock. "And you're going to be late if you don't hurry."

Shit.

Dominic headed for the shower.

He made it to the door when Lara called out, "You all have nicknames?"

"Yeah." He glanced over his shoulder.

"Yours?"

"Auntie," he said with a grin. He wasn't ashamed. He was damned good at guiding and advising, and a lovable cuss to boot.

Lara's laugh said she got it. Then her smile dimmed. "And my brother's?"

"Sir."

"Sir?" She frowned. "Because he's your superior officer?"

"Nope. He's been Sir since he joined the SEALs."

He didn't elaborate.

He didn't have to.

She called him Prince Perfect.

The team called him Sir.

Same difference.

Dominic headed into the shower wondering what the hell he'd gotten himself into.

Reuniting Lara—who was hot, sexy and incredibly fascinating, but prickly as hell with a hard candy shell—with Sir, Yes, Sir, who had no interest in connections of any kind, as far as Dominic could tell, would be right next to impossible.

But another thing Auntie was good at besides fixing everything up just right?

Doing the impossible and making it look easy.

Something to remember.

11

Wow, Lara. You have the best luck with hot guys.

Sucks about getting fired, but hey, a couple weeks of hot sex is worth it.

Of course you're welcome to crash at my place until you have a new apt and/or job.

See you next week—don't do anything I wouldn't do.

Christi

LARA REREAD THE email for the fifth time, tapping her finger on the laptop keys, but still didn't respond.

Did she have the best luck?

Or the worst?

She definitely had a pattern: find hot guy, have a wild affair, turn her life upside down. Get screwed over and left alone.

Not that she figured Dominic was going to screw her over and leave. Just because every other guy she'd been involved with had, that didn't mean he would, too. That wasn't his style. Dominic was a great guy. She might have had bad taste in flings in the past. But she had to have faith that she wasn't stupid enough to actually fall in love with a guy that wrong. Was she?

Lara glanced at the bed, images of their incredible sexy times flashing through her mind. That wasn't all they had, though. They had fun together. They had a lot in common, from fitness habits to favorite food to taste in music.

And he accepted her. No judgment, no snarky comments about her being a dancer or her dream of being a security tech.

Shaking off the weird mood, Lara saved the email without replying.

Since she wasn't sure when, exactly, she'd be back in Reno, she'd answer it after she talked to Dominic.

Not about their relationship, of course. At least, not out loud. She wasn't that needy. Nope, she just needed to find out when he was tapping Phillip for the money he said he'd owe her so she could cover her trip home.

Shaking off the feeling that she'd just put a mental deadline on her time with Dominic, Lara tapped the keys to open the final project she'd turned in that morning, wishing she still had it to work on.

She looked around the room, needing a distraction.

Before she had to look very far, she heard the hotel room door shut and grinned.

Yay. Distraction was here.

She glanced down at her jeans and light sweater, wishing she was dressed a little sexier. But hey, she could be naked in ten seconds flat, and that was sexy enough.

"Hi," she greeted when Dominic finally walked through the bedroom door. She frowned when he shut it behind him. What? He'd gone shy? "I thought you'd be tied up until evening."

"I snagged some time," he told her, grinning. "I've got a surprise for you."

Delighted, Lara smiled. This was getting to be a habit. He never had gotten around to telling her what the surprise was yesterday. First she'd distracted him, then he'd distracted her. Then, thankfully, he'd been called on duty last night, so they'd had to postpone his little friendly get-together with his buddies.

Her smile faded a little. That meet and greet was supposed to be postponed to next week. It couldn't be his surprise, could it?

"Does the surprise involve whipped cream or strawberry jelly licked off each other's bodies?" she teased, figuring it never hurt to lay the groundwork in case she needed a little distraction.

Besides, she loved the image it invoked.

Maybe he didn't, though.

Her brow creased when he gave a tiny wince.

"Not that kind of surprise." He glanced at the sitting room door, then in a lower voice added, "But you can thank me with that later if you're so inclined."

Later?

Sooner was better, but she was too curious to push. Or in this case, pull him into bed.

"Thank you for what?" she asked.

"The surprise." Before she could press for details on just what the surprise was that had him so giddy, he asked, "What's that?"

She followed his glance to her laptop, with the file sent message still blinking on the screen.

"That would be my final project. Done and gone this morning." Too excited to contain it, she jumped to her feet, wrapped her arms around him and squeezed. "I'm done, done, done."

"Hey, that's great." His smile shone with pride, sending a shaft of happiness through Lara. She'd never had anyone happy for her accomplishments before. A part of her felt self-conscious, but mostly she wanted to do a victory dance around the room. Then she wanted to strip him naked and do a victory dance on his body.

"So what happens next?" he asked.

Since she didn't figure he meant naked dancing, Lara puffed out a breath and considered.

"The final projects are all due by the end of the week, and the course ends the next Friday. Luckily, since I'm finished with all of my work, I don't need to attend any classes, so I won't get dinged for that. The instructors will assess the projects, then post the winners of the internship the next Monday."

Dominic frowned at the closed door that led to the sitting room, then dropped to the chair Lara had just vacated.

"So you get the internship, what then?"

She smiled, pleasure flooding her at his faith.

"I suppose it depends on which of the firms I win the internship with, but from what I understand, most would want me to start by the first of the month."

She tucked her hands into the pockets of the long duster-style sweater she wore over her jeans and tee, pacing the room as she thought aloud.

"I can crash with Christi for a while, but I'll need to get a new apartment, obviously. And a side job since none of the internships pay as much as I need if I'm going to put enough aside for later."

"Later?"

"Yeah, after the internship is done, I'd like enough to go out on my own. That takes money."

"You figure on taking a part-time job plus this security gig? What're you going to do?"

"Well, I'd planned on dancing, but I'm not sure how that's going to work out. Flo and Roberto will give me a good reference, but Rudy knows a lot of people, and he's big on trash talk." Lara shrugged, trying to shake off the little voice chiding her for once again letting a guy mess with her life. This wasn't a mess, she mentally argued. She'd just taken a little vacation in sexual nirvana, fallen in love and had a great time. The things she'd lost were no biggie. She'd always planned on leaving that job, that apartment, eventually.

"Huh. Well, I'd planned to wait, tell you this later, but it looks like this is the time."

"Tell me what?" Nerves jumped into Lara's stomach so fast they sent all her happy-dancing urges flying away.

"You need a job, I've got you covered."

"You got me a job?" The nerves tightened. It was one thing to chalk up losing her spot on the chorus line and her apartment as results of keeping her safe. He'd been doing that for her own good. But she had a job lined up. One she'd worked damned hard for.

"I tugged a few different lines so you could have some options." He smiled expectantly.

Lara tried to smile back, but her lips didn't want to move.

"I know you want to do security stuff, and I've talked to Lucas. He's getting me some names of companies down here that you can apply with." He paused as if waiting for her to gush her gratitude. Lara crossed her arms over her chest, waiting to hear the rest. Finally, he shrugged.

"There are other options, too. I figure with your skills, you could come on as civilian personnel. You know, work on the base. I've got the paperwork for you, everything you need."

Blindsided—but not knowing why since this was what guys always did—Lara pressed her fingers to her temple. She tried to curb her automatic reaction, which was pure anger. He was just doing it because he wanted them to be together. It was guy sweet—a nice gesture with not a lot of clear thinking behind it.

Maybe once she reminded him that she'd already put in two years to earn a top internship and that inputting data as a Navy secretary wasn't in her plans, they could get to the whipped cream.

But first…

"That's the surprise? Job connections?" She knew it sounded paranoid, but she couldn't help it.

"Nope. That's just something I figured I should tell you. Especially since the opening on base is only taking interviews tomorrow. I pulled strings to get you an appointment in the afternoon. I figured you might want to go shopping for interview clothes or something earlier."

"Interview clothes?" she echoed faintly, looking down at her favorite jeans.

"Yeah. Something girlier than jeans, but not quite as girly as your feathers." He grinned.

Lara wasn't sure if that was a commentary on the way she dressed or if he was just worried about what his peers thought of her. All of a sudden a little voice whispered in her mind, wondering if duty had canceled their outing the previous night or if he'd decided to fix her up first. She mentally rolled her eyes at the paranoid voice. Seriously, was she that insecure?

"Dominic, I really appreciate it. But…" She frowned. "If that's not the surprise, what is?"

"You ready?" he asked, looking almost as pleased with himself as he'd been the night of eight orgasms.

"I don't know," she said slowly.

"Sure you are." He wrapped one huge hand around hers and pulled her to the door. "C'mon."

Since digging her heels into the carpet smacked of immaturity, Lara let him pull her along. Slowly.

"What..." Her question trailed off as they stepped into the sitting room.

He had to be kidding.

Little black dots danced in front of her eyes and a buzzing filled her ears. Lara's feet did dig in now, as much in anger as to keep herself from falling.

Without realizing it, she shook off Dominic's hand so she could cross her arms over her chest.

"Hello, Lara."

Heart pounding, she lifted her chin in a nod of sorts.

He looked so different.

But so much the same.

He was taller. Broader. Handsome, naturally, but with a harder edge than he'd had at twenty. Maybe it was the way the white uniform set off his dark hair and gold-kissed skin.

His gaze was guarded, green eyes so like her own cool and assessing.

"Phillip," she finally said, furious when her voice broke.

This wasn't sentiment pounding through her, she assured herself.

She didn't want to cry because her brother was standing in front of her, a reminder of so many painful memories. She didn't feel horror seeing the healing bruises on his face.

Nope, all of this was righteous fury.

She tore her gaze off Phillip, aiming her glare at the other man in the room.

She'd made it clear that she didn't want a family reunion.

But apparently Dominic thought he knew better than she did what was good for her.

Lara felt light-headed, which was a good distraction from the nausea churning in her stomach.

Holy crap.

Here she was again.

Life must have a permanent parking spot labeled Lara's Screwup just waiting for her to settle in again.

A hot guy, great sex and some crazy promise of a better life and what did she do?

Run, not walk, away from every damned thing she'd worked for. And this one had not only turned her life upside down and relocated her—hello, déjà vu—but he had the unbelievable audacity to parade her long unlost brother in front of her?

Lara pressed her lips tight as she looked from one man to the other. It took all of her hard-learned control to keep the tears in the back of her throat and not pouring down her face.

Why did betrayal always surprise her?

"So?" Castillo gave a pleased nod. "What d'ya say? You want me to leave you two alone for a while?"

Deep breath.

It didn't do squat to calm her down, but Lara wasn't looking for calm.

"Lara?" Castillo's smile dimmed a little, a frown creasing his brow as he glanced from her to her brother.

Phillip, on the other hand, hadn't changed his expression—bland—or his stance—poker straight—since she'd walked in. He just stood there like a perfectly polished statue, his uniform crisp and his eyes distant.

She frowned at the bruise on his face. It wasn't fresh, more like a week or so old.

"When did you know he was free?" Her eyes didn't leave her brother's damaged face as she asked Castillo the question.

When he didn't answer, she arched her brow at Phillip.

"The team pulled me out two weeks ago," he said quietly.

"Two weeks." She swung her gaze to her lying lover. "You knew. Before we came here, you knew he was safe? That I wasn't in danger?"

"The mission was classified," Castillo said uncomfortably.

Out of the corner of her eye, Lara saw her brother's slight frown.

Classified, her ass.

"Okay, one of you say something," Castillo demanded. When they both only stared, he threw his hands in the air. "What is your problem? You're brother and sister. So talk. Yell. Hell, throw things around the room. Whatever it takes to be family again."

Lara's laugh was bitter. "Now, see, that's where you screwed up." She walked back into the bedroom to snag her laptop, then slung her purse over her shoulder before returning to stop in front of Castillo. "We were never family."

"Now, sweetheart, you're just being stubborn. Right, Banks?"

Lara followed his gaze to her brother. For a second something flashed in those eyes. Humor, regret. Hurt so deep Lara didn't understand it. Then in a blink, he went all stoic again, offering only a shrug.

Looked like agreement to her.

Lara turned to leave.

"Where are you going?" Castillo grabbed her arm, halting Lara's move toward the door.

"Away." She glanced at his hand, then gave him a chilly look. "So let go."

"You're being—" Not being a total idiot, he bit off the rest of his comment before he said something really stupid.

But Lara didn't need to hear the actual word to know where he was going. He thought she was stubborn, stupid, crazy. Since he clearly didn't think she was smart enough to make her own choices or lead her own life, she shouldn't be shocked.

Yet she was.

"Phillip?" she asked, not taking her eyes off Castillo. "Can you hold this?"

Her eyes still locked on her ex-lover's face, she held out her laptop. It was wordlessly taken.

"In the future, you might want to give a girl a little credit for knowing her own mind," she advised Castillo quietly. She clenched her fists together, one wrapped over the other. Then with another deep breath, she swung sideways with all her might to slam Castillo in the gut. Damn the man, he didn't budge. He didn't even gasp. No matter. It was the gesture that counted. "Not our future, of course. We're through."

Lara wanted to shake her fingers to release the stinging pain, but wasn't about to give him the satisfaction of knowing he'd hurt her. In any way.

She held out her numb hand, glad her fingers were working enough to wrap around the laptop when Phillip handed it back.

She met her brother's eyes. There was no mistaking the laughter in his gaze this time.

"Bye."

"I take it we're through here?" she heard Phillip say as the door swung closed.

"Not by a long shot," Castillo muttered.

"Sorry. My money's on her."

For the first time since she'd walked in and seen betrayal standing in her sitting room, Lara smiled.

Sure, it was salty from tears and wobbly at the corners.

But it was still a smile.

Uptight and righteous though he might be, her brother definitely knew a smart bet when he saw one.

DOMINIC'S SHOCKED STARE rocketed between the man standing unfazed in the sitting room and the door that Lara had just stormed through.

The door looked friendlier.

What was with this family?

First Banks argued up a storm over seeing his sister. The guy had been through a traumatic situation, between the capture, the rescue and a handful of Navy shrinks poking at his brain to see if it'd gone soft. You'd think he'd want the family connection. That he'd be grateful for a chance to fix things.

But no. He'd been a total pain in the ass about it. Dominic had had to play dirty to get him there.

Now Lara?

She'd gotten irritated that he was fixing her career issues, then she'd stormed out instead of thanking him for giving her back her brother?

This day sucked.

"Why the hell didn't you say something to keep her here?" he snapped at Banks.

"What was there to say? Your claim that I owe you got me here, despite my warning you that cozy family reunions aren't my style. From what I saw, Lara probably issued that same exact advice." Banks shrugged. "So what would you have me say? The only thing that comes to mind is 'I told you so.'"

Dominic blinked, his shock holding fury at bay.

"Did you just say 'I told you so'?"

What were they? Teenage girls?

"No. I said that's the only thing that came to mind."

Dominic ground his teeth together so hard he swore he could taste enamel. The guy was hell on technicalities.

"Don't you want family?" he asked, truly baffled by their behavior. If he'd ever seen two people more in need of connections, it was Lara and her brother. But both of them were fighting like crazy to stay alone.

"Do you always decide what other people should want?" Banks asked. The guy didn't sound mad, just faintly curious.

"When I l—care about someone, I try to make them happy," Dominic shot back, horrified by the near slip of the tongue. No *L* words here. Just a habitual response to an argument he'd had plenty of times in the past, usually with his sister. When that lame justification did nothing to calm the churning in his belly, he changed topics.

"She's not unreasonable," Dominic muttered. "If I can just get her back in here, she'll listen."

"You know her better than I do." Banks's lips twitched. "I never observed a tendency toward reason and amiability growing up with her, but it has been a few years."

Yanking the door open, Dominic paused to stare at the guy. "You're cracking jokes?"

He hadn't even realized Banks had a sense of humor. Of all times to show it off, he chose now? Dominic glanced toward the window, wondering if ice was on its way from hell freezing over.

He shook his head, giving Banks another dark look before turning to go after Lara.

"A word of advice," Banks said softly.

Impatient, brows arched, Dominic looked back.

"Lara's right. We're not what you'd call family, not by most definitions. But if you go after her, do so carefully. You hurt my sister, I might have to take steps."

"Jokes and threats?" Dominic observed, suddenly grinning. "You two really are alike."

His smile disappeared when he reached the elevator, finding its doors wide-open and no Lara. Scowling, he stared at the empty space and considered the options.

Was Banks right? When he found Lara, was she going to be reasonable? History didn't lend itself to that idea. She was the most exciting woman he'd ever known, but she was also the most difficult. He'd only had a woman run from him twice in his life, and both times it was Lara. It was enough to give a guy a complex.

Or tempt him to look elsewhere.

TIRED OF WAITING for the elevator, Lara had hit the stairwell. She figured stomping her way down twenty flights of stairs was better than beating her laptop against the elevator wall.

What the hell was wrong with her?

If a guy wasn't loser, he was a liar. If he wasn't a liar, he was a charming control freak with commitment issues and sexy dimples.

Lara had to stop at the last landing to catch her breath and wipe her face. She'd be damned if anyone, even a hotel bellboy, was going to see evidence of her heartbreak. A quick dash of her palms over her cheeks, a couple of soothing gulps of air and she was ready to go again.

She slowly made her way down the last couple of dozen steps, fiercely holding all negative thoughts at bay.

So she didn't have any money.

She'd find a bank, pull the rest of her savings to get her home.

So she didn't have a home.

Christi had already offered her couch.

She'd be fine.

She'd be miserably unhappy, living a sexless life for the rest of her existence, but dammit, if that's what it took, fine.

Bottom line, this time nobody was ruining her damned life.

Not even her.

Lara wrapped her hand around the doorknob to the lobby, sucked in a deep breath and pulled it open.

And walked right into Castillo.

Dammit.

She glared.

"What'd you do, put a homing device in my purse?"

"Actually, if I was going to fit you with a tracking device, I'd put it in your laptop. You never go anywhere without that."

She pursed her lips, not about to be dragged into cutesy banter. Instead, she waited. He'd come running after her; he obviously had a reason.

"I think you misunderstood my intentions," he finally said, his smile engaging those lethal dimples.

Yep, she did.

She'd thought he was as crazy about her as she was about him. She'd thought he understood her, that he got her. She'd thought, for the first time in her life, that someone respected her. All of her. Her body, her mind, her dreams and her heart.

She'd been too busy misunderstanding that to have a clue about his intentions.

"I don't think I misunderstood that you ignored my explicit requests and very detailed explanations of what I wanted," she told him as calmly as she could.

"So you're going to throw this away out of stubbornness?"

Chin quivering, Lara pressed her lips together, wishing

desperately for anger. Or better yet, numbness. She'd give a lot not to feel right now.

"I don't think I'm throwing anything away," she said when she was sure her voice wouldn't shake.

"Sure you are. Because you didn't like your past, now you're going to ruin your future?" He shook his head as if he couldn't understand her at all. Since Lara figured she'd been the one fooling herself to think he could, she couldn't fault his gesture.

"I don't see that my future is any different right now than it was before you dragged me away from my apartment three weeks ago," she said. Well, not much different. She was pretty sure she'd never let another man touch her. She was positive her heart was broken and her faith shattered. But those were just life's ways of reminding her that she'd screwed up.

"You have a chance at something here," he argued. "Something that's important to you."

Lara frowned. Was he trying to apologize for ignoring her wishes, for bulldozing over her plans and treating her like a stupid child who didn't know any better?

Maybe he was really bad at it.

"Just exactly what do you think I'm throwing aside?" she asked slowly, knowing it was stupid but needing to give him a chance.

"You need family," he claimed, looking and sounding as though he'd just issued a proclamation from on high. What did he figure, that she should drop to her knees in thanks?

Lara rolled her eyes, using all her willpower to keep from kicking him instead.

"You really think that's what's important to me? Seriously?"

Somewhere through her fury a little voice pointed out that it was better that he have some stupid idea of her dream than know the real one. The him-and-her-together-forever dream.

"Fine," she decided. "If you want so badly to fix me up, familywise, then okay. Let's trade."

"What?"

"I'll take your family. You can have mine."

"See, that's what I mean." He pointed as if she'd just made some brilliant point. "You're sublimating your need for family by developing an unhealthy attachment to mine."

Lara didn't realize her jaw had hit her chest until the ringing in her ears clued her in that she wasn't breathing.

She shook her head, sure she'd heard him wrong.

"I'm sublimating…"

"Look, you had a lousy family growing up. You meet mine and realize what a good one is like. It's only natural."

"You think I'm with you because I have the hots for your family?" she asked, pushing her hand through her hair in confusion.

"No, of course not. You're with me because the sex is amazing."

While Lara was trying to decide if it was pure arrogance to speak so close to the truth, he kept talking.

"But sometimes things get murky, you know? You've been through a major emotional trauma, whether you realize it or not. Your place was trashed, you were stalked, then hauled away from everything you knew. You've lost your job, your apartment and almost lost your last living relative. So of course you're clinging to my family. It's only natural."

As if his words sucked the life out of her, Lara sank back against the wall. She held her laptop against her chest like a shield. Anger drowned in the wave of hurt that washed over her. This had nothing to do with Dominic being a control freak who thought he had the answer to everything. Nor was it some deep-seated desire to reunite her with her estranged brother.

No.

This was all about him wanting to keep her away from his family. After all, he had a reputation to protect, and a clinging lover who knew his home number didn't fit that macho love-'em-and-leave-'em rep.

"You go ahead and think that," she stated. She'd be damned if she was going to stand here and defend her emotions. Not the real ones, not the stupid ones he was claiming she had.

Lara had heard enough about that thing called unconditional love and had always sneered a little.

Not now, though.

Now she understood.

She loved Dominic. She didn't need him to fit an image in her mind to keep that love. She didn't expect him to give up things or change careers or dress a certain way.

But if he had sliced a vein open and written it in blood, he couldn't have made it more clear that he didn't feel the same.

Lara had spent more than half her life not being good enough, not being accepted for who she was.

And she'd promised herself that she'd never spend another second that way.

Which meant it was time to go.

"Goodbye," she said quietly. Without waiting for his response, she stepped around him and headed for the lobby door.

"You're kidding, right?"

She didn't respond, but it only took him a moment to step in front of her.

His face was as serious as she'd ever seen it. Not focused, like the military protector he'd been. Not intense, the way he looked poised over her body. Simply serious. Lara blinked back the tears and tilted her head to indicate he should say what he had to, then move.

"You walk out, that's it," he told her quietly. "And you're too smart to do that. To throw away what we have over a temper tantrum?"

Somehow, his words made it easier. Pulling her bad attitude around her like a protective cloak, Lara shrugged.

"Like I said…goodbye."

Feeling ancient, every step filled with pain, she walked around him and out the doors.

It was like getting dumped twice.

12

LARA LOOKED UP from her plate of French fries and sighed.

"Seriously?" she asked, too exhausted to even sound angry.

"Looks like," Phillip said as he slid into the booth opposite her. He was in civilian clothes, which probably accounted for why she'd been able to eat in peace for as long as she had.

"How'd you find me? Some secret SEAL tracking technique?" Lara leaned back in the cracked vinyl booth, laying one hand on her laptop. "Did Castillo install a GPS somewhere?"

"Nah. I just hit all the McDonald's in walking distance until I found you."

Lara couldn't stop her smile as a hint of pleasure made its way through her misery.

"Old habits," she said with a shrug.

As a vegetarian and a dancer, she'd lived on health food most of her life. So she'd always headed for junk food when she was upset. Phillip had found her at one when she'd run away at thirteen, at another after a disastrous country club dance when her date had dumped her for not putting out.

Lara was pretty sure the only times she and her brother

had ever had anything that resembled personal conversations were that one Christmas and at McDonald's.

Sighing, she slid a fry-covered tray to the middle of the table as a peace offering.

"Why are you here? Did Castillo guilt you or something?"

A fry halfway to his mouth, he gave her a look that was part confusion, part amusement.

"What do I have to feel guilty about?"

"Nothing." She swiped a fry through the ketchup pool before pointing it at him. "Which is my point. But why else would you be here?"

"Castillo said I owed you some money," he told her, not looking as though the fact bothered him.

"Oh," she said, glancing down at the tray again.

It suddenly bothered Lara, though. It'd been one thing to joke about it with Castillo. It was another to sit in front of Phillip feeling like a charity case.

Then again, beggars and choosers were in vastly different categories.

"Hey, I realize it's not my place. And I'm honestly not even sure why I'm asking…." Phillip grimaced, clearly not happy.

Whether it was the question he was not happy to ask, or simply having to talk with her, Lara didn't know. Not feeling nearly as friendly anymore, she pulled the tray back to her side of the table.

His lips twitched, so he clearly got the message. But being Phillip, he ignored it. God forbid something like emotions get in the way of him doing what he saw as his duty.

"Believe me, I'm as unhappy asking as you will be answering. But right is right," he said, giving the table a careful look before he laid his forearms on it and leaned forward. "Are you sure you want to walk out on him? He seems to genuinely care about you. And I know you wouldn't have stayed here sharing a hotel room if you didn't care about him."

"He messed with my life," she said.

"And?"

Fury flashed in Lara's chest, so hot it was hard to breathe. She leaned forward so she was halfway across the table and got in her brother's face.

"I'm not some guy's project. A fun little sideline to make him feel righteous and manly while he fixes what he sees as the problems with my life. If I want changes in my life, I'm the one making them. I'll be damned if some guy is going to call my shots."

Phillip pulled a considering face, then slowly nodded.

Good. Lara leaned back, trying to even out her breathing.

Discussion finished, he could give her the money and this whole farce of a family reunion would be over.

"But here's the thing…"

Lara dropped her face into her hands and groaned.

"I'm not close to the guy, nor have I spent time with him outside of duty. But I wouldn't classify Castillo as the kind of person who looks for reasons to feel righteous." Phillip grimaced again. "If you ask me, he's already got plenty of those. His ego and his sense of worth are considerable."

Lara lifted her head just enough to peek over her fingers.

"Are you saying you think Dominic is a conceited know-it-all?" she asked slowly.

Phillip frowned for a second, then nodded.

"Yeah, pretty much. Which is why he clearly doesn't need, nor would he go looking for, a project of any kind."

"And yet, despite my saying not to, he brought you to

see me. He tries to get me to take a job that's totally outside my field and that I'd hate. Hell, he's even offering up fashion advice." Lara threw her hands in the air. "I'd say that has all the earmarks of a righteous project."

Phillip pursed his lips.

"I don't like to give advice—"

"But you'll make an exception for me," Lara interrupted.

His mouth quirked. But, of course, he got control before the grin actually appeared and gave a regal nod instead.

How on earth were they actually related?

"I feel as if I owe it to you to make an exception." He frowned, looking down at his hands. For the first time, Lara noticed the scars crisscrossing the backs of them, as if he'd been cut.

Her gaze traced the bruises on his face, pain tying knots in her belly at the thought of what he'd been through.

"Phillip—"

"As I was saying," he broke in before she could express her—what? Sympathy? Horror? Regret? She felt them all, but didn't know how to put them into words. So she lifted her hands to let him know that she'd let it go. God forbid they muddle through some uncomfortable emotional discussion. They might get close or realize they had some inkling of familial feelings.

Which would make Dominic right.

And Lara wasn't about to let that happen.

"Castillo might be a little arrogant in his belief that he knows best," Phillip said, making her lips twitch. It was like a pot describing a kettle. "But in this case, I think he had your best interest at heart."

"You think dragging me here to Coronado, knowing there was no threat, trying to play family matchmaker by reuniting us against our will, then claiming his actions were simply altruistic is having my best interest at heart?"

Phillip's expression didn't change for a few seconds, then he sighed. "Okay, if you put it that way, he sounds like an ass."

Lara snorted, then laughed so hard she could only nod her agreement.

"But ass or not, he really did seem upset when he finished talking with you earlier."

Laughter fading, Lara took a sip of her iced tea before shrugging.

"Sure, he was upset. How often is Dominic Castillo called out on being wrong?"

"Was he wrong? Or was he simply not telling you what you wanted to hear?"

Ouch.

Lara wasn't the kind to expect sympathy and hand-holding, but come on—wasn't a big brother supposed to stick up for his sibling, maybe pat her on the head a few times before gently guiding her to reality?

"I'm just saying that often, truth is relative depending on a person's perspective. I'm not defending Castillo's actions. Just suggesting that perhaps you should take a wider, less personal view of the situation."

But she didn't want to.

She wanted to be justifiably angry.

After all, fury kept the hurt at bay much better than logic. But, finally, Lara nodded.

Then, unable to let it go, she frowned at her brother.

"So, seriously…is he ever wrong?"

Phillip's grimace was a work of art.

"Let's just say that some of his arrogance is well earned." Phillip paused, then reached into his jacket pocket. Lara's mouth dropped when he pulled out a wad of cash.

"I understand I owe you. Time and a half, right?" he said, handing her the money.

"I was just needling Castillo," she protested, pushing the stack of bills back across the table. "I'm not a charity case. I don't need your money."

"Take it. If not for me, you'd still have a job, an apartment and most of your belongings."

"No, if it weren't for those goons I'd still have that stuff. And none of it is anything I can't live without." Like Phillip, she wasn't a fan of guilt games. She was happy to dump a lot of things at her brother's feet. Irritation, bafflement, maybe a little disdain. But not guilt. He had enough scars—he wasn't carrying the blame for that crap, too.

"Take it." He paused, then with another grimace, added, "Please."

Lara laughed. She couldn't help it. He looked so pained saying that precious word.

"Look, it's not much. Besides, morally you're entitled to half the Banks estate," he pointed out. Frowning, she noted that he didn't refer to them as his parents, either. Interesting.

"Legally I'm entitled to nothing," she returned with a shrug. She wasn't bitter; she'd made her choices and had no problem standing by them.

"I said *morally*." For the first time since they'd reunited that morning, maybe for the first time in her life, Lara saw regret in Phillip's eyes.

She'd never questioned his moral stand. If there was anyone who had a clear view of right and wrong, and firmly planted himself on the side of good, it would be Phillip.

She frowned, studying his face. The lines were tight in

the grooves of his mouth. His eyes, the same green as her own, held secrets. From his capture?

What had they done to him?

Lara had to glance away, knowing the sight of her tears would irritate him.

"Look, take the money. Give me your bank account number and I'll transfer more. I don't have enough liquid assets to cover half of the estate until I sell the house. But I can send enough to give you time to decide what you want to do."

"You're selling the house?" Lara asked, not really caring but needing to buy time to figure out how she felt.

"Unless you want it?"

"God, no," she exclaimed so loud the teenagers behind the counter turned to stare.

Phillip's nod made it clear he felt the exact same way.

"Why are you doing this?" she asked, truly curious.

"Does it matter?" At first he calmly returned her impatient stare. Then he shrugged. "I know I wasn't much of a brother to you when we were growing up. I'm not trying to make up for that. I figure we were a product of our environment and it is what it is. Regrets, lamenting over the past—those are a waste of time."

Lara blinked, surprised to hear her own attitude coming out of his mouth. She couldn't imagine that was something genetic—their parents had been the king and queen of using the past as a weapon. Maybe she and Phillip had more in common than she'd imagined.

"Okay," she slowly agreed, sliding her hand toward the money, but she didn't put it in her purse. Not yet. "On one condition."

"You're putting a condition on accepting money you obviously need and deserve?"

"Yep." Lara wet her lips, looking down at the tray,

empty but for a scattering of salt and a smear of ketchup. She needed a second to reel in her emotions, knowing neither she nor Phillip would be comfortable otherwise.

Finally, she met his patient gaze again.

"I'll take this, and I'll help you sort through and settle the estate if you want."

For a second he looked surprised, then relieved. Then he nodded for her to continue with her terms.

"But in exchange, you can't tell Castillo where I am." Agreement clear on his face, he opened his mouth. But before he could say anything, Lara held up one hand. "And you promise to talk to me."

He shook his head. Not in denial, she could tell, but in confusion. Lara took a deep breath and reached across the table to lay her hands over his.

"We might not really be family, and I doubt we'll ever be friends," she said slowly, putting all the sincerity she felt in her eyes. "But maybe we don't have to be strangers."

DOMINIC WHALED ON the bag, putting all his weight, frustration and aggravation behind each punch.

"Castillo."

Jab. Jab. Uppercut, right cross, jab.

"Castillo."

Fury flew from his fists.

A loud metal snap rang out.

Panting, Dominic stared blankly at the black bag as it flew across the floor, the metal stand heading in the opposite direction.

"Looks like you killed it."

"Huh?" He looked around, blinking the sweat out of his eyes, then scowled. "Lane. What are you doing here?"

"Looking for you." Brody nudged the busted punching bag with the toe of his boot. "I lost the draw."

Dominic frowned. What were he and Masters up to? The only guy smart enough to know better than to pit his ego against Bad Ass's luck with the cards was Masters— he always insisted they draw straws.

"What's the deal?"

"You're moping." Brody held up one hand before Dominic could tell him where to shove that opinion. "You've been moody, pissed at the world and a general pain in the ass for the past month."

"So?" Dominic snapped, grabbing a towel to wipe the sweat from his face. Better to see when he punched his friend.

"So when Landon started talking about having his wife chat with you, we figured we'd do you a favor and give you a chance to fix your attitude."

Dominic winced. Landon's wife was gorgeous, sweet and seriously fun. None of that made up for the fact that she was a psychologist.

"So because you drew short straw we have to have a heart-to-heart?"

"Sucks, but yeah."

"I'm heading home on leave tomorrow for my cousin's wedding. How about I work on my mood while I'm there and we skip this little chat?"

Brody looked as though he was considering it, then shook his head.

"Sorry. Duty is duty."

"Dammit." Dominic threw the towel on the bench, glancing around for something else to punch.

"How about I make it easy. I'll talk, you nod."

Dominic rolled his eyes.

"You're having lady problems. Your girl hooked you hard, then she left. Right?"

Shit.

"How d'ya figure?"

"A month ago she was all you could talk about. You were corralling everyone, wanting to do date nights and crap." Brody shrugged. "Then you stopped talking about her and started bitching about everything else."

Dominic ground his teeth. The only thing worse than this situation was everyone else knowing about it.

"Fine. I'll stop bitching."

"Too late. You triggered the Alexia threat," Brody said, referring to Landon's wife. "Now we gotta fix this."

"Hey, it's no big deal. I was hot for a woman and it didn't work out. Just as well," Dominic said with an off-hand shrug. "It's not like we had a chance anyway."

"Why? She one of your cousins?"

"Funny." Dominic debated admitting she was worse— Banks's sister. But figured that'd definitely land him on the shrink's couch.

"I'm not a serious-relationship type of guy," he said in-stead. "Military, SEAL. That just doesn't scream commit-ted relationship, you know."

"Why not?"

"I've read the stats. I've played designated driver plenty of times for guys who are drowning their heartbreak. Mili-tary and marriage, it's not a great mix," Dominic pointed out. His gaze landed on the ring Lane wore when he was off duty, making him wince. "Not knocking you, buddy. Genna is amazing, you guys are great together. I'm just…"

"Scared?"

Fury flashed. Dominic's fist swung before his brain engaged.

Shit.

He realized what he was doing an inch before he made contact with Brody's face. At the same time, his friend's hand whipped out.

His hand wrapped over Dominic's fist, Brody arched one brow, then gave a slow, pitying shake of his head.

"You pulled that, Auntie. You throw a punch, you better put a little more effort into it. Otherwise you'll end up flat on your ass."

"I remembered at the last second that I didn't want to hurt you."

Brody laughed. "Right, you go ahead and tell yourself that if it makes you feel better."

Dominic yanked his hand away, resisting the urge to shake off the sting. Hard to believe the guy had been out on medical leave a few months back. He had a grip like a vise.

"Landon takes a dim view of fighting among the ranks," Dominic added, knowing it was lame but figuring it was better than admitting he'd lost his cool.

He never lost his cool.

Something else to blame Lara for.

Right along with his poor sleeping, lousy appetite and nonexistent sex drive. At least, as it applied to other women. In the month since Lara left, he'd had plenty of sexually driven thoughts about her. But the second he considered taking those thoughts elsewhere? Nada. It was unmanning how fast he went from firm to fail.

"Damn, Bad Ass, you suck at consoling," he said, feeling crappier than he had before he'd beat the hell out of the punching bag.

"Next time we play five-card stud," Brody muttered as they both turned toward the door.

"What'm I missing?" Genius asked, sauntering into the gym.

"Auntie here is sharing his wisdom on the topic of doom and gloom as it befits the military and marriage," Brody told Masters with a grin.

Hell.

Dominic dropped to the bench, resisting the urge to drop his head into his hands, as well.

Dominic stared at those hands instead, surprised to see the knuckles scraped bloody. He glanced at the bag, wondering how long he'd been punching without feeling a thing.

"You ever worry that you're gonna disappoint?" he asked quietly. "That you're in this relationship that makes you feel good—light and happy, you know? But that you're chaining her to something that's not."

"Not what?" Brody asked.

"You think we carry a heavy load with our job, that we work in the dark, that it dims that light?" Masters said, that genius brain of his getting the metaphor.

Dominic shrugged. He didn't like this asking for advice thing. He was the go-to guy. The one with the answers.

Having to ask someone else just wasn't right.

Neither was depending on someone else to be there. Wishing someone would take on the craziness of his career and want to stick around.

"How do you guys do it?" he asked, the desire to find a way to make it work overcoming his frustration.

Masters and Brody exchanged glances, both looking equally uncomfortable. That made Dominic feel better for some reason.

"You just do it," Brody mumbled, kicking at the weight bench. "You know, if it matters, you make it work."

"You figure it out, that's all," Masters said with a shrug, looking around the gym as if it'd recently been decorated with pictures of naked chicks.

"How?" Equally curious and starting to enjoy his friends' discomfort, Dominic leaned back. "Seriously. You love your ladies enough to commit, right? So how do you balance it? How do you keep from feeling that you're screwing them over?"

Damn.

He grimaced, irritated that he'd let his amusement loosen his mouth. That wasn't the kind of thing he meant to share. Hell, that wasn't the kind of thing he even wanted to admit to himself.

But neither of them looked confused, surprised or even amused at the question. They both looked deadly serious. Thankfully, neither started spouting crap about quality time, unconditional love or, God forbid, sexting for long-distance fun.

"Don't ask me," Brody said, lifting both hands. "I tried to quit once and she damn near threw beer bottles at my head. Genna says she's proud of what I do. I think that helps."

"Sage had a chance to play the quit card with me. She wouldn't do it, though," Masters added, his expression proud. As if his lady had done something amazing.

And she had, Dominic figured. Both of them had a shot at marrying a normal guy, one who was around most days and nights. One who didn't have *top secret* written over half his career.

Would Lara feel that way?

He tried to imagine Lara saying she was proud of him, but the image just wouldn't compute. Had she ever indicated that she was proud of him? Pretty much her only reference to his career had been when she'd been cussing at him for dragging her out of her apartment.

Somehow Dominic just couldn't picture her as a sweet little stay-at-home military wife, doing tea and bingo in base housing with the other wives.

"You guys got lucky," he told them with a rough smile.

"You sound like you don't think you'd have the same luck," Brody observed.

"It's not his luck he's doubting. It's my sister."

Dominic barely contained his groan as he got to his feet. Could this day get any worse?

As one, the three men turned to the door. Brody whistled under his breath while Masters gave a pitying shake if his head.

"You're hooked on his sister?" Brody muttered.

"Dude," Masters chided with a laugh.

"Castillo?"

"Sir?" Dominic returned, automatically shifting to attention.

Banks tilted his head toward the door.

Masters paused long enough to give Dominic a punch to the arm, Brody offered a pat on the back, then they were both smoke. Banks had that effect on people.

Dominic jerked his shoulders, shaking off the automatic battle tension. The guy had a right to voice his thoughts when it came to his sister.

"You have a minute?"

Frowning, Dominic nodded. It wasn't the request that confused him. It was that Banks would make it. He wasn't known for asking. Or chatting, for that matter.

"Sure. You here to chime in on the chances of a military guy having a lasting relationship?'

"Of course not."

"You're not going to offer me advice?"

"Me?" If Dominic had asked him for a kiss smack on the lips, Banks couldn't have looked more shocked. "Hardly. Besides, I thought advice was your forte."

"Advice takes one of two things," Dominic observed. "Experience or objectivity. This is a situation in which I have neither."

"Well, don't look at me." For the first time, Banks didn't seem like a windup military machine. The guy appeared so seriously horrified that Dominic had to laugh.

"Okay, so if you're not here to offer advice, what's up?"

"I want to talk to you about Lara."

Dominic's smile faded. He widened his stance, just in case.

"Landon takes a dim view of fighting among the ranks," he pointed out for the second time that hour.

Not that that'd stop him. He figured he owed Banks a few brotherly obligation shots. And he wouldn't mind taking a couple of his own. Nothing personal, but the guy had been a witness to Lara dumping him. A few gut shots might soothe the ole ego.

"Why do you think I'd be looking for a fight?" Banks asked. He didn't sound obnoxious or confrontational. Nope, just curious. The man was a mystery.

"Lara?" Dominic left it at that. If the guy didn't have his own list, he wasn't stupid enough to provide one.

"I'm pretty sure if my sister wants your ass kicked, she'd prefer—and is totally capable of—doing it herself."

"Yeah, she is." The woman was seriously built and damned strong. And he knew for a fact that she could—and would—fight dirty.

"You know, I'm not here to take you down, but you start thinking lusting thoughts about her while I'm standing right here in front of you and I might change my mind," Banks mused.

"Fair enough. I'll save my lusting thoughts for later," Dominic said with a grin. Damned if the guy wasn't kinda funny.

"You do that. In the meantime, why don't you tell me what you're planning?"

"I thought you weren't here to offer advice."

"That sounded like a question to me."

Dominic squinted.

"Are you asking my intentions?"

He waited for the laugh. He got a nod.

Holy crap.

"Okay, I get that you're within your rights as a brother, but seriously? The first time you talked to her in eight years was a month ago. Do you think Lara would appreciate you sticking your nose in her business?"

"That'd be between her and me, wouldn't it?"

"And this is between her and *me*."

"No. You met her through my situation." Banks's pause was infinitesimal, his wince barely there. But when Dominic caught it, his fury fled. The guy had been through hell and his hell had almost caught his sister. He had every right to be angry. "You brought her here, you orchestrated a meet between us. That makes this between her and you and me."

"Okay. So what do you want me to say?" Dominic asked. "That I'm sorry? That I made a mistake? Or that I'm crazy about your sister?"

All of which were true.

"Nope. Like I said, I'm not here to offer advice. I'm just warning you—don't fuck with my sister. She's got a chance to start over now. If you choose to be a part of that new beginning, you'd damned well better plan on being a long-term part. You don't plan on sticking it out, then let it go."

Dominic wanted to protest the ultimatum. He wanted to ask if the guy knew where Lara was, how she was doing. He wanted details on this new beginning and where she'd be making it.

But he was still stuck on the fact that uptight, upright Lieutenant Banks, code name, Sir, Yes, Sir, had just said *fuck*.

It was mind-boggling.

Banks didn't wait for a response, though. Message delivered, the guy was done. With a nod, he stuck his cap back on his head, executed a smooth about-face and strode out of the room.

Leaving Dominic with one inescapable fact: he and Lara were either over for good, or he'd better man up, admit his feelings and figure out if he could handle them.

He sank back onto the bench, his shoulders sagging and his head throbbing.

He sorta wished Banks had belted him in the face instead.

13

DOMINIC STORMED UP the path to his cabin, wondering how many new levels of pissed he could reach before his head simply exploded.

He'd wasted two days of his leave on a wild-goose chase, then gotten his ass chewed out by his brother for not returning the truck sooner, then by his mother for missing so many of the wedding festivities.

That's why he was pissed, he told himself.

He didn't like being bitched at. When he'd told Lucas that, his brother had taken his truck keys and advised him to walk his sorry self home. The only reason Dominic hadn't planted his fist in Lucas's face was that their mother had been standing there, nodding.

He dug into his pocket for the remote to disarm the alarm, then stomped up the steps.

His hand on the doorknob, he stopped.

Emotions slammed into him, the images of the last time he'd been home flying through his head in mocking clarity.

Lara.

Damn.

Where the hell was she?

He'd gone back to Reno. She didn't work at the ca-

sino, she didn't live at the apartment, she didn't attend
the school.

He'd called Lucas a dozen times, asking him to run her,
but apparently big brother was too busy.

He'd even called Banks, who'd straight up laughed.

Nobody could—or would—tell him where Lara was.

He shoved the door open, determined to pull strings
and tap one of his cousins to run her when Lucas wasn't
around.

Just inside the cabin, he stopped short.

The scent hit him first, an instant turn-on with floral
overtones.

Then he saw her.

Lounging on his couch, looking comfortable and happy.

And so damned good.

Lara?

What the hell?

"What are you doing here?"

She didn't seem surprised to see him. If anything, her
expression was satisfied enough to cross over into smug.

"Visiting," Lara said, crossing one stocking-clad foot
over the other. "Your mom figured I'd be more comfortable here than up at the house."

"My mom…"

"Yeah. Your grandma sent down enough food to turn
me into a beach ball, though. So I've been going to the
gym with Celia. Matteo is going to teach me to ride horses,
too, but I didn't figure that'd compensate for homemade
tortillas."

"You took over my house? My family?" He'd looked
everywhere for her, and she was right here? He'd driven
for twelve straight hours, gotten a speeding ticket and been
hit on by a redhead named Flo whose age was somewhere
between fifty and a well-preserved ninety. He'd been fran-

tic, sure he'd lost Lara for good. Sure he'd ruined the best thing in his life he wasn't positive he wanted.

All the time, she'd been here.

His head was spinning. Dominic didn't know if he should grab her, strip her naked and celebrate finding her again. Or grab her and shake her crazy.

Either way, he wanted his hands on her—fast.

"I told you, I'm visiting."

"Don't you usually let the host know you're visiting?"

"Right," she said, laughing. "Like you'd have let me stay here without bugging me if you knew where I was."

"You realize you just proved my point, right?"

Her sigh was a work of art. And it did amazing things for the black sweater she was wearing. Which he told himself he wasn't noticing. He refused to let himself get distracted by sex. His body didn't agree, but Dominic figured he had enough anger to override its wishes.

"You're grumpy," she observed before leaning over to lift a plate from the coffee table. "Want a churro? Your aunt dropped them off this morning. She made them for the wedding and had extras."

"My aunt…" Dominic couldn't take it all in.

She'd claimed his paranoia about her using him for his family had been a lame attempt to push her away. And she'd been right.

Yet here she was in his house. Spending more time with his family than he did. Dominic didn't think he'd ever been this confused in his life.

"Look, you said you thought I was using you. You said you thought I had some deep-seated need for family. So I figured I'd try yours on and see if you were right."

"This is an insane invasion of privacy," he said, throwing his hands in the air as he paced from one end of the room to the other.

"Like you're one to talk?" She laughed. "You hauled me off under false pretenses, kept important information from me, then tried to run my life. All I did was sleep in your bed."

Images of Lara in his bed did a tempting dance in his brain. Dominic stopped pacing so fast he was surprised his feet didn't kick up smoke.

No sex, he reminded himself.

Not even in his imagination.

Dominic forced his thoughts back on the straight and narrow, promising his body an ice-cold shower if he could get through this without grabbing Lara.

"Seriously. Why are you here?"

Lara sucked her bottom lip between her teeth, sending his thoughts flying right back to the image of her, naked on his bed. Dominic almost groaned.

"You ignored everything I said. I told you about my career goals and I told you how much I'd hated my upbringing," she said quietly, looking at her fingers instead of at him. "I opened myself up to you. So when you blew off my feelings, it hurt me."

God.

Dominic scrubbed his hands over his face, two days' whiskers scraping his skin.

He'd been such a jerk.

"I know. I'm sorry," he told her. Whatever happened between them—and he figured it'd probably be goodbye—he owed her that. "I figured it out the day after you ran away."

"I didn't run away," she snapped, hurt clearing from her face as she glared. "I told you I was leaving. And if you knew, then why didn't you do anything? Why'd you wait a month to find me?"

"You think I haven't been trying?" This was it. This was what was going to push him over the edge. "I was on duty, which means I can't traipse off chasing a woman who tells me we're through. I left messages, though. I called the casino. I talked to your brother. Hell, I even went by your old apartment."

She got to her feet, tucking her fingers into the front pockets of her jeans while she frowned.

"You went to Reno?"

"Yesterday."

"That's why you're late for the wedding?"

"For the fourth time today, the wedding isn't until Saturday. I'm not late," he ground out.

"So why'd you go looking for me?" she asked.

"Why don't you tell me why you're in my house?" he shot back.

"You first." When Dominic just glared, Lara wrinkled her nose and shrugged. "I was back east, but I figured we had some things to settle between us. And Lucas had invited me to the wedding, so I figured this was as good a time as any to settle them."

"You were back east?" New York? Was she thinking of going back to dancing? Dominic wanted to protest that she had worked too hard to give up on being a security tech, but figured he'd interfered enough already.

"I went back to Maryland," she told him, her features drawn as she stared out the window. He knew she was seeing her past rather than the changing colors of the trees outside. "I had some stuff to take care of there."

"Closure?"

"What?" She frowned, then pressed her lips together. He thought she might be about to cry until he noticed the humor dancing in her eyes. "Um, not emotional closure. I had that when I ran away."

"So why'd you go back?"

"To help settle the estate. Phillip has been doing it all

long-distance, but there were things that were better done in person. So I did them." She bit her lip, then admitted, "Maybe that is a form of closure? Not with my past, but between my brother and me."

"You cut ties with Banks again?" He wanted to protest. To tell her that a guy who would issue threats on his sister's behalf was one who might be okay. Maybe. Again, he'd interfered enough already. But damn, keeping his mouth shut was hard.

"No, I didn't cut ties with him. We just closed that chapter of our lives. What comes next depends on how hard we try, I suppose."

"Try what?"

"Try to be family," she admitted, wrinkling her nose. "You were right about that."

He wanted to grab her, hug her, confess his feelings then haul her off to bed.

But he didn't.

He couldn't.

Because while she'd been unwilling to admit her need for family before, he'd been unwilling to admit his real fear.

"I'm a SEAL, Lara. Do you know what that means?" Of course she didn't. Hell, his own family didn't know the extent of the danger he lived with regularly.

"Are you asking if I know what your career means?" At his nod, she added, "In general? Or to you specifically?"

"Either. Both."

"Does it matter?"

Yeah.

Yeah, it made all the difference in the world.

If she could handle his career, he'd gladly hand over

his family, his house, his heart. If she could accept him for who he was, what he was, he'd happily give her everything he had.

LARA DIDN'T KNOW where his worries over his career choice had come from, but she supposed it was a fair question. After all, she'd gotten all freaked thinking he wanted to change hers. And not that she trivialized what she did, but it in no way compared to the dedication and focus his job took. She knew some of what he did on duty was crazy scary. Then again, so was life sometimes.

So she gave his question the weight it deserved. She thought for a second to be sure she knew how to put her thoughts, her feelings, into words.

"Starting with the big picture, I think the SEALs are pretty amazing. Not only because of how well you're all trained or how talented you are at doing the impossible. But because you put your lives on the line every day to protect your country." She took a deep breath, not sure why she suddenly wanted to cry. That kind of dedication was heart wrenching. "I didn't value much of what I had growing up, because it was always used as a stick trying to whip me into shape. But my grandfathers served our country. I heard their stories, I saw their pictures."

His half nod told her he understood her ingrained respect.

Okay. Lara wet her lips. Now it got more personal.

"And then there's your team. You serve with guys who, from what you've told me, aren't just incredible SEALs, they are great people. Fun, interesting, strong. I was afraid to meet them," she confessed.

"Why?" He looked shocked.

"Because they are so important to you. Because I know their opinions matter. These are the guys who protect you, who cover your back. They're the guys who saved my brother. I owe all of you more than I can ever say, and that scares me," she admitted.

"I wasn't there," he reminded her.

As if it mattered.

"No. You were keeping me safe so your team could rescue him. But you have been there plenty of times in the past. Rescues, missions to eliminate terrorists, covert operations."

"You've been watching the Military Channel," he muttered.

Lara laughed a little.

"Sure, I wanted to know more about what you do. I did research, too. Comes in handy, my ability to hack websites."

"You didn't..."

"Hack the government?" She'd been tempted. "No. I figure you're doing your part to keep the country safe. The least I can do is not jeopardize that."

"So you admire the breed." He crossed to the window, staring out for a second. "But doesn't mean you're comfortable with it on a personal level."

"Are you comfortable with me being a showgirl?" she asked.

"Sure, if that's what you want to do." He gave her a confused look before he shrugged.

"A lot of guys wouldn't be. You've said it yourself—I'm showing my all up on stage. I know what's going through the minds of the guys watching. The message is sex and when I'm up there dancing I use my body to send it."

He nodded, but still didn't look as though he understood. Lara loved him so much for that.

"Some guys, they'd get all jealous or possessive. They think that if their girl is up there dancing, she's as good as charging by the hour. Or they figure what she's got is theirs and theirs alone."

"Some guys are idiots."

"Yeah." She grinned, glad hers wasn't. "But you don't care. And now that I'm in security, if I take on a job that requires me to carry a gun, to maybe play bodyguard, would you be okay with it?"

He blinked at the sudden career shift, then gave it a second while he considered. Frowning, he asked, "Are you getting training before you go out? Not in the security stuff. I already know you're aces there, because of all of Lucas's praise. But you haven't worked with guns or physical security before, have you?"

As much as an unconditional *woo-hoo* would have gratified her ego, Lara liked that he was being cautious, because that way she knew he really believed what he said.

"No," she said, answering his question. "But I'm being trained by someone really good."

"Who?" He lifted his hand. "Not saying I don't trust your choices, I'd just like to know the person training you is solid."

"Lucas."

"Lucas? Castillo? My brother?" For a second he looked as though he'd just taken a fist to the gut. Then Dominic's face shifted, a grin slowly emerging. "That's why he's been dodging me and wouldn't help find you. He knew all along because he convinced you to come on board with Castillo Security, right?"

"Right," Lara said slowly. She was cringing inside, not sure she could defend her decision if he got pissed. She still wasn't sure she could defend it to herself. She'd tied herself and her career to the family of a man who might very well toss her out on her ass and hate her forever.

But this time she'd put everything on the line by choice.

She shifted, lifting her chin and pulling back her shoulders. This time it was her decision. It wouldn't suck any less if it blew up in her face. But at least she'd be the one calling her shots.

Maybe life, in its infinite wisdom, would kick down a reward for that. Or at least stop messing with her.

She tried to find comfort in her choice, but her stomach was threatening to rebel and her nerves were so tight she felt as though she was about to snap.

Especially when Dominic just stood there, staring.

"Well?" she finally prodded. "Say something."

"I'm thinking."

"Think faster."

He grinned.

Then he stepped closer.

Not close enough to touch, thankfully, since Lara wasn't sure she could resist. But close enough that she could smell his cologne, that she could remember the scent of it on her skin.

She slowly blew out a breath.

"You're working with Lucas. That means you're being trained by the best," Dominic said slowly. His tone gave weight to his words, letting her know how sincere he was. "You gave up your internship for this?"

She couldn't tell from his expression how he felt about that. So she answered the smartest way she knew how—she sidestepped.

"So you're okay with my occasionally being in danger. With me having a career that I might be a little obsessed about." She tilted her head toward her ever-present laptop. "I'll have client confidentiality clauses, too. So I wouldn't be able to talk about some cases."

"That's all a part of the job. I've seen it plenty of times with Lucas's and the cousins' work," he said with a shrug.

Lara waited. The guy was crazy smart, so the fact that he didn't see the correlation told her how worried he was about her accepting his career.

Finally, needing to touch him and knowing she couldn't the way she wanted to until they'd settled this, Lara stepped close enough to poke him in the chest with her index finger.

"So you'd be fine with it?"

"Yeah, sure," he shrugged. "I'm not saying I wouldn't worry from time to time, depending on what you were doing. But I know you can handle yourself and I'd support you while you did."

Lara looked away, not wanting him to see her tears. But oh, God, she loved him so much. She had to take a deep breath, then another, before her eyes stopped burning and she could look back at him.

"Everything you just said, that's how I feel, too."

His eyes lit, then the light banked a little as he couldn't quite believe her.

"You want to clarify?"

"That's exactly how I feel about your job. You're extremely well trained, you're surrounded by an incredible team who are all focused on not only succeeding, but on covering each other while they do." She lifted both hands as if to say, *what else was there?* "I'd miss you while you were away, of course. But the rest, I'm fine with it."

He looked dumbstruck.

"You're serious? You're totally comfortable with my being a SEAL?" he asked, not sounding as if he could quite make himself believe her.

"Would you quit if I wasn't?" She knew it was a mean question, but Lara couldn't stop herself from asking.

From the look on his face, though, it wasn't one Dominic wanted to hear. His grimace was pained as he shoved his hands into his pockets. He didn't physically step away from her, but Lara felt the distance.

"I couldn't," he said quietly. "I can't quit being who I am. I can't turn my back on what I believe in."

Lara was pretty sure she'd gotten teary eyed more times since he'd accosted her outside the casino than she had the entire rest of her life. She had to blink fast to keep the tears from falling.

"I'm sorry," he said quickly, reaching out to lay his hand on her cheek. "I wish I could change that. It's all I've thought about the past month. But I just can't if I want to live with myself."

"But that's just it," she said, sniffing. "I wouldn't want you to. But you understand how hard it would be for me to give up my dreams, my goals, for you."

His eyes narrowed before he closed them and groaned. "You walking out, that wasn't really about me pushing you into meeting with your brother?"

"Well, a little. You have a habit of running roughshod over choices when you think you're right." She wrinkled her nose, knowing that wasn't going to go away. But somehow, knowing it was because he cared—and dammit, because he was usually right—she figured she could live with it. "But it didn't feel like you were giving me the support you, yourself, want."

Looking disgusted with himself, Dominic shook his head.

"I wasn't. I couldn't get past the idea of you leaving long enough to see what I was doing, though. And if I had, I was still sure my career would be an issue."

"It's not," she promised.

Lara wanted to dive into his arms. She wanted this to be finished now so they could get to the makeup sex. But as much as she wanted all of that, she wanted this to be a fresh start. That meant clearing up everything.

She grimaced.

"What?" Dominic asked, peering at her face.

"You said you thought I was using you to fill some deep-seated—and apparently deeply hidden—need for family. So I thought I'd better figure out if you were right."

"I thought you said I was using that as an excuse," he muttered.

"Oh, I still think that," she told him. "But I don't use people, so it bothered me that you thought I would. And I like your family and the experience I'd had with them enough to actually wonder if you were right. So I had to find out."

"And?"

"And…" Lara's voice trailed off.

This was hard.

She knew what she wanted. She knew she was strong enough to make it work. But it was still really, really hard to say it out loud.

She'd been on her own, unencumbered by family, for eight years.

They'd been lean years, filled with heartbreak, disillusionment, fear and a hand-to-mouth existence that sometimes still terrified her. But they'd been better than being Lara Banks, daughter of Randall and Ellen, sister to Phillip the perfect.

Now she knew who she was, and she knew what she wanted.

She wanted Dominic.

She took a deep breath, stepping back a little. Not far, just enough that she wasn't touching him.

She needed a little space for this.

"And I found out that while you have a great family, I

do have a family of my own. So as much as I enjoy yours, I don't need them."

"Wait, what? You have a family? You mean Banks?" Dominic's expression was a combination of triumph and irritation. "You and he have been building a bridge? And he never told me? He let me dangle, even when I asked point-blank if he knew how I could find you."

Arching one brow, Lara waited.

Dominic grimaced.

"Sorry, fine, you were saying what you want."

He sounded so grumpy she almost smiled.

This was it. Everything she'd thought she wanted in life she'd wanted alone. She'd spent years keeping distance between her and others, terrified to open her heart to rejection.

But she couldn't have it all unless she took the risk.

And with Dominic, she wanted it all.

"I want you," she said, keeping it simple.

Then Lara held her breath.

She'd never been so scared.

She'd never cared about anything as much as she did Dominic's response. She'd survive without him. She was strong enough to know that.

But, dammit, she didn't want to.

Dominic's smile settled every fear, though. The ones she'd admitted and the ones she'd been afraid to let surface.

"You got me," he said, finally pulling her into his arms. "But you should know, I've had enough of you walking out. You take me and it's for good."

Lara wrapped her hands behind his neck, pulling his head down to brush a soft kiss over his lips.

"Deal," she whispered.

"I love you," he said, resting his forehead on hers and looking so deep into her eyes, Lara was sure the declaration was imprinted on her soul. "I love you, and it's forever."

She couldn't stop the tears from falling this time. Not when they were happy tears.

Laughing through them, she kissed him again, sliding her tongue gently over his before pressing whisper-soft kisses against his lips.

She leaned back, both hands on his cheeks. She wet her lips, waiting for the fear. But there wasn't any.

Because this was right.

"I love you, too," she said with tremulous smile. "I really love you."

Forever.

* * * * *

Would you like to read more sexy SEAL stories?
Want to find out if Phillip Banks can
find a woman to love him?
Look for #819 CHRISTMAS WITH A SEAL
by New York Times *bestselling Blaze author*
Tawny Weber,
available in November 2014.

#815 WICKED NIGHTS
Uniformly Hot!
by Anne Marsh
When local bad boy SEAL Cal Brennan threatens to put
Piper Clark's dive shop out of business, she'll do anything to
take him down a notch. Including proposing a sexy bet where
the loser takes orders from the winner for one night...in bed.

#816 SOME LIKE IT HOTTER
by Isabel Sharpe
California free-spirit Eva and her Manhattan sophisticate twin
sister agree to swap coasts and coffee shops—to perk things
up. When busy exec Ames Bradford makes stopping by a
nightly habit, Eva's soon brewing it up hot and satisfying!

#817 CLOSE UP
From Every Angle
by Erin McCarthy
Kristine Zimmerman is finally divorcing the man she left years
ago. Sean Maddock is even hotter now but there's nothing left
between them, right? Then he proposes a deliciously sinful
weekend for old times' sake...and she can't think of a single
reason to refuse.

#818 TRIPLE THREAT
The Art of Seduction
by Regina Kyle
Playwright Holly Ryan's Broadway dream may come true with
the help of sexy blockbuster star—and former high school
crush—Nick Damone. The heat and intensity between them
might set the stage on fire!

REQUEST YOUR FREE BOOKS!
2 FREE NOVELS PLUS 2 FREE GIFTS!

HARLEQUIN

Blaze

red-hot reads!

YES! Please send me 2 FREE Harlequin® Blaze™ novels and my 2 FREE gifts (gifts are worth about $10). After receiving them, if I don't wish to receive any more books, I can return the shipping statement marked "cancel." If I don't cancel, I will receive 4 brand-new novels every month and be billed just $4.74 per book in the U.S. or $4.96 per book in Canada. That's a savings of at least 14% off the cover price. It's quite a bargain. Shipping and handling is just 50¢ per book in the U.S. and 75¢ per book in Canada.* I understand that accepting the 2 free books and gifts places me under no obligation to buy anything. I can always return a shipment and cancel at any time. Even if I never buy another book, the two free books and gifts are mine to keep forever.

150/350 HDN F4WC

Name	(PLEASE PRINT)

Address	Apt. #

City	State/Prov.	Zip/Postal Code

Signature (if under 18, a parent or guardian must sign)

Mail to the Harlequin® Reader Service:
IN U.S.A.: P.O. Box 1867, Buffalo, NY 14240-1867
IN CANADA: P.O. Box 609, Fort Erie, Ontario L2A 5X3

Want to try two free books from another line?
Call 1-800-873-8635 or visit www.ReaderService.com.

* Terms and prices subject to change without notice. Prices do not include applicable taxes. Sales tax applicable in N.Y. Canadian residents will be charged applicable taxes. Offer not valid in Quebec. This offer is limited to one order per household. Not valid for current subscribers to Harlequin Blaze books. All orders subject to credit approval. Credit or debit balances in a customer's account(s) may be offset by any other outstanding balance owed by or to the customer. Please allow 4 to 6 weeks for delivery. Offer available while quantities last.

Your Privacy—The Harlequin® Reader Service is committed to protecting your privacy. Our Privacy Policy is available online at www.ReaderService.com or upon request from the Harlequin Reader Service.

We make a portion of our mailing list available to reputable third parties that offer products we believe may interest you. If you prefer that we not exchange your name with third parties, or if you wish to clarify or modify your communication preferences, please visit us at www.ReaderService.com/consumerschoice or write to us at Harlequin Reader Service Preference Service, P.O. Box 9062, Buffalo, NY 14269. Include your complete name and address.

HB13R2

Twin Temptation!

California free spirit Eva and her Manhattan sophisticate twin sister agree to swap coasts and coffee shops—to perk things up! When busy exec Ames Bradford makes stopping by a nightly habit, Eva's soon brewing it up hot and satisfying....

Don't miss

Some Like it Hotter

From reader-favorite author

Isabel Sharpe

Available October 2014 wherever you buy Harlequin Blaze books.

HARLEQUIN®
™

Blaze®

Red-Hot Reads

www.Harlequin.com

HB79820